Going For Bronze

By

Gio Lassater

Cover design by TatteredWolf Studios
Interior design by Gio Lassater

ISBN-10: 0692370994
ISBN-13: 978-0692370995

Also available in eBook format at Amazon.com.

I'll be a park, and thou shalt be my deer;
Feed where thou wilt, on mountain or in dale:
Graze on my lips, and if those hills be dry,
Stray lower, where the pleasant fountains lie.
~ William Shakespeare

Chapter One

J'd spent two months trying to find the entrance to the dragon's lair. Two months sailing around that damn island, diving from the ship to find an underwater cave that could lead to the entrance. Bronze dragons have only one way in and out of their lairs. It's an ocean cave with a tunnel usually long enough that only a dragon can survive swimming through. Humans don't have the lung capacity.

This tunnel leads to a lair, which is usually inside of a volcano. I knew that bronze lived on the island I'd been circling because I'd followed him from the port city of Nwansk. Unfortunately, I'd not been close enough when he had dived below the ocean surface to find his cave.

Until now.

"Ok, I'm ready for you to cast the spell." I turned to the mage I'd brought with me.

Arvon dug some things out of the satchel slung over his shoulder, bade me drink a nasty black liquid that had the consistency of pitch, and started mumbling something that could have been a recipe for biscuits for all I knew. Within a few seconds, he finished his recitation, and I threw up all over the deck.

When I pulled myself together, I stripped down to my small clothes. With a strip of leather, I tied a small bag of pearls to my waist. Arvon nodded his head, I jumped in the ocean, and when I sucked in water, I didn't drown. Lucky for me.

During my swim down toward the ocean floor, I sent a silent prayer to my sister, Genev, who at that very moment lay dying of some unknown malady. It was for her that I sought the dragon.

I hoped that it would have some concoction, potion, or spell that would help me heal her. I knew myths and legends that surrounded dragons, and thought I'd heard one or two that concerned healing. I didn't know for sure that the bronze would be able or even willing to help me, but I had nothing to lose.

I have no idea how long it took to reach the cave. At first I thought I'd made a mistake, but once I saw past the coral and boulders that obstructed the entrance, I quickly made my way inside and started the long swim toward the dragon's lair. It didn't take as long as I thought it would thanks to the currents pushing me. In almost no time, I saw light ahead, and I pushed onward, closer and closer to the end of my ordeal.

As my head emerged from the water, searing heat pummeled me. If I'd been breathing, I'm sure my lungs would have burst into flames. I guess the lava was closer to the entrance than I'd imagined it would be.

I stepped from the water, and my skin dried almost instantly. Attempting to push aside the temporary discomfort, I made my way onward and upward, following the massive tunnel toward the beast's home.

My hand strayed to the bag at my hip. Pearls are a favorite of bronze dragons. Favorite treasure. Favorite snack. I guessed either way I should be set to pay the dragon for its services.

Ahead, the tunnel began to widen slightly, and then suddenly it opened into a massive chamber that could have held an armada. Piles and piles of pearls, gold coins, and glistening coral stretched as far as the eye could see. The only thing I didn't see was the dragon.

I cursed softly and started into the chamber. The dragon's treasure cascaded away from me as I slogged through it, up one mound and down the next. I made enough noise that if the creature was home, it would know someone was here.

"What the hell do you think you're doing?"

I suppressed a scream, and looked all around me. "Show yourself, dragon. I mean you no harm."

Laughter reverberated through the chamber, and only then did I realize that the voice and laughter were human, not dragon. Although...I'd never heard a dragon speak or laugh before, so maybe I was wrong. My hunch quickly proved out as a man popped his head above a pile of gold coins. He continued laughing, wiping mirth-induced tears from his eyes. He walked toward me.

"What's so damned funny?" I asked.

"You, you daft moron. 'I mean you no harm.'" He tripped over a rather large piece of coral when another fit seized him, but instead of being angry, he only laughed harder because of it. "Like a dragon is going to be afraid of you. Have you ever seen a dragon, boy?"

I bristled at being called "boy," but his laughter had me down right furious. "Whether I have or have not seen one is none of your damned business. I came here to seek the dragon for my own reasons. Reasons that are of no concern to you."

He pushed himself to his feet and closed the distance separating us, all the while attempting to hide the smug smile that still haunted his face. "Please forgive me. It's been a while since I've had anyone but the dragon for company. His sense of humor tends to run in a vein that most humans would find off-putting. I meant no harm or disrespect."

He stopped in front of me, and I got a truly good look at him for the first time. And that look was more than enough to take my nonexistent breath away. Eyes the color of azure seas, filled with glee, stared into my soul and took its measure. His hair, as black as hell itself, cascaded down his back, framing shoulders that should have been on a deckhand. A body the gods had sculpted from the finest marble in the world, olive and glistening from the heat.

"Have you come to rob the dragon?" His eyes continued to bore into me, and I knew that he would know if I lied to him.

"No, as a matter of fact, I brought these as payment for a request I want to make." I loosed the thong that held the bundle of pearls to my waist. The proximity of the handsome stranger caused my member to swell, and I attempted to distract from my predicament by opening the bag.

He whistled softly at the sight of five white and one black pearls. "Aye, that would get him excited—if he was here."

My heart nearly stopped beating. "No, no, no. He has to be here. I've been searching so long. He has to be here." I fell on my knees, clenching dragon treasure in my fists. From behind, I felt gentle, soft hands grasp my shoulders.

"Now, now. Obviously, a mighty important errand brings you to this place. Tell me what it is. I might be able to help," he said.

"It's my sister, Genev. She's gravely ill, and I sought out the dragon so that he might heal her, if it's in his power to do so. He's her only hope. Without him I'm afraid she'll die." My sigh echoed from the walls, filling my ears with the sound of despair.

He kneeled beside me and pulled me to him, laying my head in his lap and running his fingers through my short brown hair as he made soft shushing noises.

I have no idea why I allowed myself to be treated that way, but his eyes and the tone of his voice seemed to melt everything away. There was only he and I in the world, and he cared about my troubles. It was comforting.

"Don't lose hope. I know there are a few potions here that may help," he said. "I don't think he'll mind if we take them, as long as you leave the pearls in their place."

He stroked my hair and smiled warmly. I tried to apologize for my weakness. He leaned down, pressing his lips to mine, quieting my words.

Instead of being alarmed by his forward—and presumptuous behavior—my arms reached around his neck, pulling him closer to me as his tongue forced its way into my mouth. He cradled me with his right arm while his left hand explored my body.

His fingers trailed over my stomach and slipped into the confines of my small clothes. Silky, smooth flesh slid along my shaft, tugging me to instant erection. I gasped, pressing my lips against his to stifle a scream of pleasure. My orgasm ripped through my body and covered my face, chest, and his hand. My whole body turned red with embarrassment.

"Well, that was certainly impressive." He grinned.

"I'm sorry. It's just been so long," I said. "And you're so damn gorgeous."

He laughed, wiping my seed from my face and rubbing it into my chest and stomach. "It's okay. I guess I made a good choice this time." We stood as one, him supporting me until my legs stopped wobbling. "We should go."

I followed him to the nearest wall. "If you don't mind the question, why are you here?" I asked as we made our way over more dragon treasure.

"I'm a scholar. Of various things. The dragon lets me come and go as I please. He has vast knowledge that he puts at my disposal, and we keep each other company." Kradyn reached the cavern wall before I did and stooped down, grabbing two bottles from a pile of old coins. "Take these," he commanded, bending down to grab two more bottles.

As we made our way back to the watery entrance, I asked, "How are you going to get out? I doubt you can hold your breath that long."

"Don't worry. I'll be fine." Near the mouth of the cavern he grabbed a satchel and slipped all of the potions into it.

"Oh, by the way, I'm Ruldaan," I said.

"A pleasure. Kradyn."

The water felt soothing as we plunged into it, leaving behind the sweltering heat of the lava-warmed lair. We fought our way through the current, taking much more time than I had on in the inbound journey. When we cleared the tunnel, I turned to see if Kradyn was with me.

I started my ascent when I felt my lungs begin to burn. They wanted me to take a breath. Panic raced through me. I kicked frantically toward the surface. In the back of my mind, I knew I wouldn't make it.

Kradyn must have sensed my urgency and need because I felt his hands under my arms, dragging me upward. My lungs screamed, my mind screamed, and my heart hammered away in my chest. Blackness filled the perimeter of my vision. Soon it swallowed me.

Chapter Two

J awoke on the deck of my ship, coughing, sputtering, and vomiting seawater. A hard hand battered at my back, forcing me to continue coughing. Pushing myself onto my knees, I looked up to see Kradyn frowning down at me.

"Well, that was a bit of fun. All out now?" he asked.

I nodded dumbly, attempting to find my feet and get away from the ichor that covered the deck. "Thank you for saving me," I sputtered.

He waved away the words. "Not worth thanking. I only did what anyone would do. We should have a healer look at you. Make sure all the water is out so that you don't get sick."

I ordered my first mate to set course for the port of Nwansk. As he ran to the helm, shouting orders for the sails to be unfurled and to weigh anchor, I turned to Arvon, who had been standing mutely by the entire time. "Do you have a potion or spell that'll help?"

He stared at Kradyn, never saying a word, nor seeming to realize that I'd spoken to him. Several attempts later, he finally pried his eyes from the man and looked at me.

"What's the matter with you?" I asked.

He glanced back at Kradyn, and then, clearing his throat and visibly pulling himself together, he said, "Forgive me. I thought I knew him, but I was mistaken. That man died ten years ago due to a spell gone awry."

I looked at Kradyn, who smiled at the mage. Not an open smile, but a small, knowing smirk.

"As for spells or potions," Arvon said, "I believe that I may have something in my cabin. And, good news, this one shouldn't make you throw up."

I laughed in spite of myself and accepted Kradyn's assistance walking to my cabin at the aft of the main deck. Unlike the rest of the crew, who slept in hammocks strung between beams, I had an actual bed. Not much, mostly just big enough for me to sleep almost comfortably. The rest of the small room was occupied by a small square table and two chairs. Half of the wall that comprised the stern of the ship was colored, leaded glass.

Kradyn deposited me on the bed, and shortly Arvon entered with a vial of bright green liquid. "This should be just what you need to stave off any lingering effects of near-drowning." He handed me the vial, which I quickly unstoppered and drank. I'd learned never to take the time to smell or contemplate the ingredients in these vile concoctions.

"That should do the trick," Arvon said. "You'll sleep for a while. You relax, and I will ensure that First Mate Biddon has us at Nwansk with proper speed." The mage cast one final furtive glance at Kradyn, and then quickly exited my cabin. Kradyn, sitting on a corner of the table, smiled and dipped his head in Arvon's direction.

"So, does he know you?" I asked, as I slipped beneath the blankets of my bed.

Kradyn helped me to situate myself comfortably in the bed. "I've known many people in my life, so possibly."

"That didn't answer my question," I said, suddenly yawning and feeling drowsy.

He chuckled. "It's an answer, nonetheless. The only one that I can give at this time. You have my word that nothing bad will come of my being on this ship or in the presence of your mage friend."

I forced my drooping eyes to remain open. "Back there…in the cave. When we, well…you know."

A smile lit his entire face. "Ah, you mean when we became better acquainted with one another?" He laughed again.

I smiled. "Yes, that. It was amazing. You truly are beautiful."

"Thank you, Ruldaan. I'm pleased you think so." He leaned down and kissed me. I was so sleepy that it took me a few seconds to realize what he was doing and to join in. Nevertheless, I did so passionately, and when he pulled away, the smile that lit his face made his beauty that much more unbearable. "Fear not, we two shall get to know one another again."

I turned toward the bulkhead as Kradyn exited my cabin. I heard him mutter something, but sleep claimed me before I could ask what he'd said.

∞

I awoke to a rather loud commotion coming from the deck over my head. Groggily I stumbled toward the door. Throwing it open, the noise assaulted me with its ferocity, and the sound of all hands on deck running my direction had me concerned something terrible was happening. When the ship suddenly listed to starboard, I caught myself on a barrel and fought to keep my feet under me. Several men slid along the deck.

Kradyn's voice, loud, booming, and full of commanding authority, reached my ears. "Everyone stay back. He means no harm." As I made it to the stairs leading to the helm, he said, "Anyone who attacks him will answer directly to me!"

With that threat looming over their heads, all the men stopped dead in their tracks and turned to me. Being captain just became interesting. I made my way up the tilted stairs, noting that Kradyn was talking to a small bronze dragon that had perched on the rail at the aft of the ship. Of course, small was a relative term, in that the dragon was bigger than a horse and carriage together, and had jaws big enough to swallow any man on my crew without hitting a tooth.

"Kradyn, what's going on?" I asked as I slowly approached.

The dragon turned its head toward me, appraising me and my movements. Obviously it felt that I offered no threat because it turned back to Kradyn, who looked at me.

"This is Rofek," Kradyn said, "and he is assisting me with researching cures for your sister. He has just flown back from Nwansk with a report on her condition."

My heart swelled with the knowledge that he had gone to such lengths to aid my family and me. "What has he discovered?"

"I *can* talk, you know." Rofek glared at me. "Humans are so arrogant. How can you stand being around them? I feel like roasting him for a snack."

Kradyn laughed. I failed to see the humor. "Now, Rofek. I'm sure that Ruldaan meant no disrespect. He's just not used to dragons the way that I am."

Rofek grumbled, sneered at me, and then pushed himself into the air and flew quickly off to the horizon. The ship righted itself amid shouts and everyone except Kradyn grabbing onto something solid for support. I exhaled loudly and turned back to my crew.

"Everyone stand down. Return to your duties." There were many evil eyes cast in Kradyn's direction, but he ignored them, and the men slowly went about their business. "So what news did Rofek have of my sister?" I asked.

"Let's discuss that in your cabin." He brushed his thigh against my exposed cock.

I looked down, only now realizing that I'd been nude the entire time. Kradyn laughed at my discomfort. I made a hasty retreat to my cabin, and the gorgeous scholar followed, laughing the entire way.

In my quarters, Kradyn eyed me lustfully as I quickly pulled on a pair of breeches. "A pity," he muttered, shaking his head.

"How long have I been asleep?"

"A few days," he said. When he saw the shocked look on my face he said, "Arvon's potion was a little more potent than he thought it was. Anyway, Rofek says your sister's malady is unlike anything he has seen before. He believes that it's magical, not biological."

The words slowly sunk into my skull. "Someone did this...on purpose?"

Kradyn gave me a heart-felt look of sadness. "It would appear so. And, please forgive my saying this, but I find it hard to believe that you're so astonished...Your Majesty."

"Ah, so now you know," I said. "It's not like I was keeping it from you. Hell, we only met a few days ago. But, you're right; I guess I shouldn't be that surprised.

"Genev has been betrothed to Prince Zadron of Feldrick since her birth," I said. "Zadron's family has been allies with my family for only fifty years. Before that we were bitter enemies. This marriage was arranged to cement our bonds of friendship. Someone obviously has other plans."

"Arvon thought so, too, which is why I had Rofek fly him to Feldrick so that he could speak to Prince Zadron on your behalf. I hope you don't mind," he said. "He told me he's your advisor."

"It's fine. That'll save time." Pouring myself a cup of ale, I downed it thirstily and poured another. "Does Rofek know a counter-spell?"

"I'm afraid not." Kradyn reached out, snatching the cup from me and drank. "I've asked him to go to the Great Library at Elemkur. The High Wizard of the Moon is a long-time friend of mine. He'll find the answer, or else it can't be found."

Kradyn slumped into one of the wooden chairs. After gulping down a large portion of ale, he passed the cup to me. I thanked him and finished off what he'd given me. After sleeping and not eating for two days, the alcohol had me feeling tipsy and happy. A goofy smile plastered itself to my face as I admired Kradyn's body.

"You have done so much for me. I don't know how I could ever thank you," I said.

He stood up and pressed his body to mine. "I can think of a very good way—Your Majesty."

I blushed and realized I did that constantly whenever he turned the conversation or my thoughts to things more carnal. "You don't have to refer to me that way. We are—I hope—friends. You can call me Ruldaan."

Slowly he lifted his hand to my face, gently tracing his fingers along my cheek and jaw. The touch was so slight that it sent shivers through my spine. A smile tugged up the corners of his mouth.

"You're so beautiful," he whispered. "Your eyes shine like pearls."

His fingers moved slowly back up my jaw and then brushed along first one eyebrow and then the other. The whole time I stared at him, feeling the heat of his presence. Wanting so badly to touch, I forced that desire down, teasing myself and dragging out the sense of eroticism I felt from denying myself the feel of his flesh beneath my hands.

Bringing his other hand up, Kradyn held my head between his silky-soft palms and slowly moved his lips to mine. The smell of the ocean overwhelmed me as his lips fluttered against mine, moving slightly side to side. Fire and ice ran through my veins. I shuddered and gasped and felt myself sagging into his arms.

He caught me, pulling me to him, crushing me to his chest as his lips met mine in an explosion of passion and built-up desire. His tongue forced itself into my mouth as I wrapped my arms around his neck. We kissed for what seemed an eternity, and then he released me.

Before I could open my eyes, I felt his hands at the ties to my breeches, and then he was tugging them over my hips, letting them fall to the floor. My erection slapped against my stomach before he grabbed it, falling to his knees and swallowing me to the base in one breath. I felt his nose brush against me as his hands grabbed my ass. A finger roughly shoved into my crevice, finding the tight ring of my sphincter.

I gasped, reaching back and grabbing his hands. "No, you mustn't!" I cried. I jerked back from him, pulling my cock from his throat. "You can't do that. Please."

He looked at me, puzzled. "I'm sorry, Ruldaan. I thought that you wanted—"

I pulled him to his feet, staring into his eyes as I placed my hands on his chest. "I do, Kradyn. I want you more than you can possibly know, but I cannot have you in that way. It's…complicated."

Kradyn placed his hands atop mine. "As you wish, my king." He winked when he said that, and I relaxed. "Can you explain?"

"I want to. Really I do, but I—. It's—"

"Complicated. I heard." Kradyn kissed me again and then stepped back. "I apologize for my actions. I'll comport myself as a gentleman in the future." Before I could say another word, he walked out of my cabin, gently closing the door behind him.

Who says it's good to be the king?

Chapter Three

I stood, looking dumbly at the closed door that separated me from the man I was quickly falling for. It had all happened so fast. Maybe the feelings of gratitude for what he had been doing for me and my family were overwhelming. Maybe it was not anything at all, but lust or infatuation. No matter, my heart still felt the pain of his leaving. I'd hurt him. Even through his smile, I could see the pain my rejection had caused. How could I explain that I'd just saved his life?

As I bent over to pull up my breeches, a loud pop reverberated through the cabin and a rush of displaced air slammed into me. Quickly I jerked the breeches over my hips, ready to defend myself. I knew the signs of a teleportation spell.

"Arvon! What are you doing back so quickly?" I rushed over to the mage and helped him steady himself.

He smiled his gratitude at me. "Prince Zadron is hastening to your sister's side. He left as soon as I delivered the message regarding Genev." He paused, looking around the room. "You are well?"

Releasing him, I sighed and plopped down on a wooden chair, grabbing the pitcher of ale and draining the last drops into a cup. "As well as can be expected. Things got out of control. I almost forgot to stop Kradyn before…well, you know."

"Indeed, I do," he said. "Your Majesty—Ruldaan—I know that it's difficult for you, but we'll find a way to overcome your situation, too. No spell, no matter how powerful the caster, is without its flaws. We *shall* defeat it."

I nodded, more out of habit than agreement. How many times had we had this conversation? I'd lost track. I could just kill the bastard who had put this curse on me.

"What a family," I muttered, sullenly. "My sister is bewitched by some unknown malady, and if I have sex with anyone…"

Arvon cleared his throat.

I drained the ale from the cup. Standing up, I went about my cabin gathering clothing and pulling it on. More presentable now than I'd been when I met Rofek, I moved toward the door. "Come, let's find First Mate Biddon and Kradyn and determine what we should do. We'll be mooring in Nwansk harbor this evening. We must have a plan"

∞

I sat at the edge of Genev's bed, holding her pale hand in mine. Fever wracked her body, and she muttered continually. On occasion she would cry out, pain coursing through her body, sending her forward away from the pillows backing her, only to collapse a few seconds later.

"She's getting worse," Mother lamented, pulling back the curtains surrounding the bed. She stared down at her youngest child, holding back tears that threatened at the corners of her eyes. "Who could be so monstrous?" She looked at me then, and I could see the dark circles beneath her eyes. "I'm going to lose her, aren't I, Ruldaan?"

Releasing my sister's hand, I made my way to the other side of the bed and took Mother in my arms. "Don't say things like that. I'll take care of this. I promise."

I felt her body jerking as the tears finally broke through and sobs controlled her. I let her emotion run its course before I held her back at arm's length. "Go; get food and rest. If you don't, you'll be the next one in need of medical aide."

Mother nodded, giving me a weak smile. She kissed me lightly on the cheek and then left me alone with Genev.

I strode to the window, staring down on the gardens that Genev loved so much and where she spent much of her courting time with Prince Zadron. Already I knew that if she died I would have the whole lot slashed down and turned over into the soil.

A throat cleared behind me, and I looked up as a servant stated, "Your Majesty, your lady sister has a visitor." At my nod, the servant allowed Prince Zadron into the chamber.

He barely spared me a glance and nod before he rushed to his beloved's bed, taking her hand in his. I gave them time alone, choosing instead to look out the window and mull over the plan that my compatriots and I had discussed while still at sea.

Arvon, Kradyn, and Biddon walking into the room interrupted my thoughts. I motioned for Zadron to come over, and after—he thought—surreptitiously wiping tears from his eyes, he joined us at the window.

"Rofek sends word from the Great Library at Elemkur," Kradyn stated without preamble. "The High Wizard of the Moon has been able to scry the past. It seems that Genev has been cursed by a sorcerer named Tymon."

"No," I hissed. "No, not Genev, too. That bastard!" I punched my fist though a pane of the window.

Kradyn immediately pulled me back, staring at me in shock as he jerked my hand up to see. Bits of glass dug into the flesh, and blood ran quickly and freely over the stone floor.

Arvon wasted no time in calling for a cleric-healer, and Biddon helped Kradyn pull me farther from the window. I screamed my frustration, flinging my hand out. Blood splattered across the wall and Biddon's face. I'd been unable to keep Genev safe, and now she was going to pay for my mistakes.

"Calm yourself, Ruldaan," Kradyn said.

"What is going on?" Mother came stomping into the room, pushing Biddon aside. She gasped when Kradyn held up my bloody hand. "What in the Name of the Mother did you do that for?"

"Tymon." When I uttered that one word, the color drained from her face.

"Cleric, see to my son," Mother commanded. She turned to Kradyn. "Do you see within yourself the capacity to love my son?"

Kradyn nodded his head. "I definitely find myself inclined to protect him and cherish him as a great treasure."

"Men," she muttered. "Three days together, and you think you love someone. If you ever find out what true love is—and I guarantee you that it's not something that you find at the end of your penis—I suspect you just might die."

"Mother!"

"Oh, shut up, Ruldaan. Let the cleric see your hand. Already the servants are going to have a time getting your blood out of the stone. Foolish child." Mother ordered everyone out of the room, with the exception of Kradyn and the cleric. I could see that Zadron thought of refusing, but a look from Mother sent him hastening after my first mate and mage advisor. "Once you have seen to my silly child, Cleric, you, too, may leave."

The man nodded his head, bowing it at the same time in a feat no one could accomplish except in the presence of Mother. His ministrations quickly ended, and he made for the door and sanctuary beyond.

Mother looked from me to Kradyn, her gaze boring into us. Neither of us could keep eye contact with her. Finally giving one last "tsk," Mother walked over and took my wounded hand in hers. She inspected it closely, talking to herself about commending the cleric-healer for such fast and fastidious work.

"Better?" she asked, forcing me to look in her eyes. "Good. Now, I assume that you share this man's feelings?"

I nodded mutely.

"I see." She sat on a small settee at the foot of Genev's bed and arranged her skirts. I knew she was formulating her words, and I resisted the urge to flee the room. "Ruldaan, you know that I don't care who my children love. That's why I whole-heartedly support Genev marrying Zadron. I can see how they cherish each other.

"Your father never wanted his children to be used as pawns for alliances and treaties," she said. "He wanted you to know freedom, as well as obligation. I'm by no means disparaging what you might feel for this man, but you must be sure that it's not just lust or infatuation. We can ill afford another such dalliance."

Mother turned her steely gaze on Kradyn. "Though I can see how that would definitely turn your head." She smiled softly, and I thrilled in the fact that he was blushing this time, not me.

"Now then," Mother said, "if you truly care for him, I suggest that you give him all the information he needs to make an informed decision in regard to your little…problem."

I looked at Mother, and Kradyn looked at me. I didn't want him to know, and Mother knew it. Nevertheless, she was right. If I intended to pursue Kradyn then I had to be honest.

I kissed Mother on top of her head.

She patted my unbandaged hand. "Take Kradyn and have a long talk with him. When you're finished, return here, and we'll finalize your plan."

I led him outside to the gardens whose demise I'd been planning only minutes earlier. Finding Genev's secret hiding spot, I gently forced Kradyn onto the little bench that she used while Zadron read his notes and poetry to her.

I found it very humorous as Kradyn's massive frame dwarfed the tiny piece of furniture. My smile faltered when I remembered what I had to tell him.

"I'm going to tell you a story…"

Chapter Four

"Happy birthday, Your Highness," the Grand Magus said. He held a small box out for me. It was exquisitely beautiful—ivory scrollwork inset with gold filigree and emeralds that shone like green fire.

I held out my hand, and he placed it gently in my palm. "It's magnificent. Thank you."

He bowed deeply before saying, "Pardon, but the true gift is inside the box. You may open it whenever you wish."

I looked at Mother, who nodded, and I carefully unlatched the lid and pushed it up. Inside was a tiny scroll, which I unrolled and read silently. Confused, I looked at the Grand Magus.

"It is a spell," he said. "I crafted it especially for you, and it will aid you when your heart is most in need. Keep it with you always, for you never know when that time will come."

"Thank you." I bowed slightly to him to show him the true scope of my appreciation. I replaced the scroll and set the box on the arm of my chair near Mother's throne.

After the Grand Magus stepped down from the dais, musicians began to play rousing music, and the apprentices from the school of magic streamed down the center aisle. Their colorful robes—denoting the years of training they had completed—made no noise. I didn't know if that was through magic or not.

The head of the procession stopped short of the dais, his black robe with a golden hem swirling around his ankles. The remainder of the students lined up on either side of him. When a single line had been formed, they all bowed as one.

"Your Majesties, it gives us great honor to perform for you this evening." The lead student turned toward me and bowed again.

"Especially for you, Prince Ruldaan, in celebration of your birthday."

I inclined my head to him.

The crowd quickly pressed against the walls while jockeying for the perfect position to take in the show. Torches were extinguished until the room was in near darkness. I could sense the guards moving closer to my mother, father, and me.

Without warning, a massive column of fire erupted from the center of the room. It licked at the stone ceiling. Ladies and not a few lords gasped or shrieked. I knew it wasn't real because I couldn't feel heat from the flames.

The lead student stepped into the center of the column, then one by one the other students scooped handfuls of the flickering light into their palms. On cue, they thrust their hands skyward. The flames joined in a long ribbon overhead and burst with an inaudible pop that showered sparks and flowers all over the room.

The audience applauded vigorously.

With the exception of one man in blue robes, the group of students separated to opposite sides of the room. The lone student, a man roughly my age with short blond hair, an aquiline nose, and gray eyes, bowed. The orchestra began to play a soft ballad.

Swaying side to side, the mage moved his hands in an intricate pattern, and before our eyes a diaphanous man and woman appeared before him. They bowed to one another, grasped hands, and began to dance in time with the music.

For several minutes we watched enraptured as the mystical duo moved about the room. Finally, as the music slowed, they separated, bowed to each other, then to the dais, and then they disappeared.

The entire time I had watched the young man while his hands moved in a pattern I could never mimic. The look on his face bespoke a concentration and a joy so deep that I was certain he would weep from it. It was, well, magical in every sense of the word.

As he bowed a second time, I inexplicably found myself leaving my seat and walking toward him. The room became deathly silent, and when the mage stood up straight to see what was going on, he locked eyes with me. Immediately, he averted his gaze and fell to one knee.

"Please, rise," I commanded. "Anyone who can do something as magnificent as that deserves our adoration."

"Thank you." He bowed again.

I heard a throat clear behind me, and I glanced at Mother. She gave me a knowing look, and I realized I was holding up the show. Stretching out my hand to the young mage, I asked him to accompany me. Together we walked from the room, and I showed him to a balcony overlooking the ocean far below.

"Your hand is very warm," I said.

"It's from the magic," he said.

My personal guards stationed themselves near the entrance, giving us our space. The light of a waxing gibbous moon bathed the stones in eerie shadows, which my guest gathered into his hands. I smiled in wondrous astonishment when he handed me a bouquet of black roses.

"That is truly amazing." I smelled them. "They're real!"

"Of course, Your Highness," he said. "Another gift for your birthday."

"Thank you." I placed the roses onto the parapet, keeping my hand on them so the wind wouldn't blow them into the raging tide below. "Forgive my manners. I'm Prince Ruldaan."

"I know, Your Highness," he said without making me feel stupid. "My name is Tymon. It's a pleasure to make your acquaintance."

I looked back at the guards. "I give you permission to stop bowing and calling me 'Your Highness.' Please, call me Ruldaan."

"Very well, Your—Ruldaan." He smiled shyly. "I'm sorry. This is my first time at court. It's all very overwhelming.

I squeezed his shoulder, amazed at the solidity I felt there. Most mages were frail wisps waiting to blow away in a slight breeze, but Tymon felt as strong and sturdy as the stones beneath our feet.

He looked at my hand then cast a smile at me. "Are you always so familiar with your entertainment?"

I laughed. "Well, some entertainment I am." I blushed. "I'm sorry. That sounded really bad. Please don't think unkindly of me."

He reached out his hand but stopped when one of the guards moved forward. Tymon backed away, bowing low and holding his hands to the side.

"He's fine," I said. Without looking I knew the guard had resumed his post. "Tymon, it's fine. Stand. Please."

Slowly he followed my request, and I moved closer to him, placing his hand on my shoulder. We both looked at the guards, who had not made another move. I winked at Tymon.

"I'm sorry," he said again.

"Another request—stop apologizing. Oh." I suddenly realized my roses had disappeared. "I'm very sorry, Tymon. I've lost your gift."

"It happens. Besides, I can always make you more," he offered.

"I would like that, but some other time. Can you stay long, or do you need to return to the school of magic?" I asked.

"There are rules I must obey, however, I'm certain they can be relaxed for a royal request," he said.

I spoke to one of the guards who left to summon the head of the school. When he arrived, clearly out of breath from hurrying to my location, I made my request. The old mage quickly and gladly gave permission for Tymon to be late for curfew or even spend the night away as long as he made his morning classes. I gave my word he would.

"So, what would you like to do, Ruldaan?" Tymon asked.

I moved close, leaning my elbows onto the parapet, and whispered, "I would rather show you what I would like to do. Would you accompany me to my chambers?"

"Of course, my prince." He placed his hand atop mine, and I marveled again at the heat. "I'm your willing servant."

I led him past the guards, who followed us only as far as my chamber door before assuming a post on either side of it. I pulled Tymon inside, closed the door more forcefully than I intended, and nailed him to it with a fiery kiss. Our lips crushed against each other, and my tongue thrust into his mouth.

Tymon's hands were everywhere, spreading their heat from my neck to my arms all the way down to my ass, which he groped with abandon. Unfortunately, the fabric of his robe was too thick for me to get a good feel when I groped his crotch, but I knew soon enough I would behold him, naked and glorious.

I broke the kiss first, panting like a race horse who'd just won. "That—you are amazing. This is going to be the best night of my life."

Tymon smiled and grabbed the back of my neck. He kissed me briefly before licking my lips. He never closed his eyes but stared into mine the entire time. I saw passion there I hadn't seen before.

"Come to the bed," I said.

Near the bed, we stood apart, admiring one another with smiles on our faces that most wore when drunk. Tymon wasn't an overly handsome man, but it was his mere presence and the power I knew that flowed through him which attracted me.

"Did you cast a spell on me?" I meant it to be a playful tease, but I saw instantly that I'd wounded him.

"I would never do that!" He stepped back, and the hurt in his eyes gouged into my heart. "Your Highness, I should leave. I don't want you or anyone else to think I would use magic to get to you."

He turned and made it halfway to the door before my body responded. I ran after him, placing myself between him and the exit.

"Tymon, wait, please. I'm sorry. It was said in jest, not as an accustion," I said. "I don't believe for a second that you have bespelled me in any way. It was a terrible, hurtful thing I shouldn't have said. Please, I beg you to forgive me."

He took a deep breath. "I forgive you. I just ask that you realize how that accusation, even said as mirth, could result in me being put to death—especially since you're now the Crown Prince."

"I do," I promised. "I knew as soon as I said it how wrong it was. You have my word it won't happen again." I kissed him to seal my words. "Now, if you wish to leave, I won't hinder you. However, if you stay, I'll more than make it up to you."

His stern visage morphed into a smile that melted my heart. "Gladly."

"Excellent." I pulled him back to the bed. "I want to see what you look like under those heavy robes." He reached for the belt at his waist. "No. I want to unwrap my present."

"Very well." He threw his arms out to the side and his head back. "I am yours, my prince."

"Well, I thank you," I said. We both laughed.

Grasping the heavy cord belt, I slowly tugged at it until it came loose in my hands, and I tossed it to the floor. Curiosity suddenly overtook me, and I realized I was wondering what mages wore beneath their robes. I was about to find out, and the realization drove me mad with desire.

I wanted to rip the fabric from his body, but I resisted. The opening of the robe formed as I pulled the separate sides, and Tymon's body presented itself to me. It was truly a gift befitting a future king.

The robe fell to the floor, leaving him standing in nothing but his slipper-shoes. His body was well muscled and covered with a light dusting of blond hair that appeared almost transparent. My breath caught in my throat beholding him. He was magnificent.

And the cock on him! Even flaccid its girth and length were impressive, and the thought of having it in me caused me to instantly harden.

"You're not disappointed?" he asked.

"By the gods, how could I be when you look the way you look?" I was truly astounded that he didn't realize what a desirous body and temperament he possessed.

"I wasn't always a mage," he said. I heard sadness and timidity in his voice that didn't deserve to come from such a man. "I was born on a farm."

"Well, I'm not complaining, believe me." I could tell my words lifted his spirits. Slowly descending to my knees, I allowed him to brace himself on my shoulders while I removed his slippers. Resting my backside on my feet, I stared at the slowly engorging flesh before me.

"You shouldn't be on your knees," Tymon protested quietly.

"How else would I do this?"

Without warning, I wrapped my hand around the base of his cock and sucked it into my mouth. Tymon gasped, and he suddenly hardened to full size. I choked when the engorged head hit the back of my throat and kept going. Backing off, I swirled my tongue repeatedly around the head.

Tymon shouted and began shuddering, his balls contracted, and I felt the warm rush of liquid in my mouth. Backing off, I allowed the final bursts to splash against my lips and licked away the salty sweetness of his essence.

"I'm so sorry," he stammered while still shaking uncontrollably. "This is—" Another spasm cut off his words, and he fell sideways on the bed. "This is my first time," he panted.

"There's no shame in that," I assured him. "Do you have another one in you?"

"Without a doubt, my prince." He stood up and drew me to my feet. "I believe it's time we got you out of those clothes."

I mimicked his actions and stood so he could do the job for me. His fingers, so adept at weaving spells, moved nimbly from button to button on my tunic, and it soon joined his robe on the floor. He pushed me onto the bed, removed my boots, and then began pulling on the ties that bound my breeches.

I gasped when he stopped and ran his palm over the outline of my growing erection. "If you continue that I'll soil my clothing."

"I would rather you soil my body," he said.

He continued the task of undressing me, and once I was naked, he stood staring down at me, drinking in the sight of my body. I blushed under his scrutiny.

"You are amazing, Ruldaan," he said. "I'm so lucky you have chosen me to please you."

I sat up, pulling him on top of me. "You're not here simply to please me, Tymon." I kissed him. My cock nestled between the solid globes of his ass, and the friction from his back and forth movements sent me quickly toward the edge.

"I want you in me," I said. I sat up, running my hands over the solid peaks and valleys of his stomach muscles up to his chest. His nipples were rock-hard, like the rest of him, and I playfully bit them in turn.

"Well, I want you in me," Tymon said. He pulled me into a kiss so I would stop abusing the tender nubs on his chest.

"We can take turns," I offered.

"Me first." Tymon slid from the bed. A line of spit dripped from his mouth onto my cock, causing it to twitch. With gentleness that bordered on torture he grasped my dick firmly in his warm hands, tugging it up and down as he worked his spittle all over it.

When it was slick, he leaned down and kissed the head, licked it, then took it into his mouth. I clenched the coverlet in my hands, hissing a curse word I'd heard frequently on the docks. I writhed on the bed as he took more and more of me into his mouth.

He gagged and retreated. Another attempt to get more of me into his mouth failed, so he settled for bobbing up and down on what he could comfortably take. We would work our way up to more.

"You have to stop. I'm close," I warned him.

He gave my cock a couple tugs while smiling slyly at me. "I need you in my ass, not my mouth."

"Come up here and get on your knees," I commanded.

He did, and I positioned myself behind him. I spread his legs and buried my face in his ass, running my tongue around the tight, virgin ring. I worked my spit into him, ensuring he was well lubed. Tymon forced himself backward, fucking himself with my tongue.

"Are you ready?" I asked.

"Yes."

I positioned my cock where my tongue had been, rubbing it up and down across his hole. Finally, after Tymon begged me to enter him, I started slowly pushing in. When the head breached the outer wall of his defenses, he moaned and filled his mouth with the coverlet, biting down on it.

I stopped to give him time to adjust to the sensation he'd never experienced before. His hole quivered around my invading battering ram, bringing me closer and closer to filling him with my royal seed. Willing myself to hold out, I resumed my assault.

By the time my balls collided with Tymon's he was sweating and moaning into the coverlet so loudly I feared the guards would burst into the room to investigate. He reached beneath himself and through his legs, massaging my balls.

"You want me to cum already?" I asked.

"No," he whimpered. "I never want this to end."

I lay on his back, kissing and nibbling at his ears. "You feel amazing. So tight. Are you ready to get fucked?"

"Yes, my prince." He sighed and released his grip on my balls.

I gently bit his ear and pulled a few inches of cock from his greedy hole. I thrust back inside him, relishing his moans. He beseeched me for more. With increasing momentum, I withdrew more and more and forced it back inside him until my rhythm had pushed me to the point I was giving him the full length repeatedly.

Tymon screamed my name, and I forced his head into the coverlet to stifle his more vociferous cries. He soon lost himself to the feeling of having his most intimate space violated and began bucking back toward me. Our flesh slapped together, echoing from the stone walls, vying with my own grunts.

He was driving me mad with lust.

Finally, I could withhold no more. I drove my cock all the way in, shouting, "I'm cumming, Tymon," while my royal seed catapulted into his hole. He screamed into the coverlet, continuing to buck beneath me. I forced him to hold still when his movements became painful against my now-sensitive member.

I collapsed atop him, fighting to get my breathing under control. He moaned repeatedly, using the muscles inside himself to milk the last drops of me. When I softened enough, my cock slid from him and drew some of my seed with it.

I collapsed onto my back. Tymon fell onto his stomach. His moans never ceased.

When the air held nothing but the scent of love making and silence, I asked, "Do you have the energy to go at me?"

He moved to lie beside me, draping an arm across my chest. "I will do as my prince desires." He kissed my cheek.

"You're amazing, Tymon. That ass of yours deserves to be loved and worshiped." I reached over and inserted a finger into him, wiggling it around.

He moaned softly into my ear. "You almost made me lose control of my magic."

With my finger still inside him, probing the wet, messy recesses, I rolled onto my side. "What happens if you lose control?"

"I don't know," he said. "That's why most mages don't have sex. It breaks down our barriers."

"Should we tempt fate by having you fuck me?" I asked.

His sphincter clamped onto my finger. "I would risk it, if you would."

I kissed him gently. "To have your cock inside me, I would tempt the very universe to stop existing."

"You are bold, indeed, my prince." He winked at me. "I want you on your back."

I removed my finger, pulled my knees to my chest, and said, "Your wish is my command."

He moved around behind me to get into position. "I have never done this before. What should I do?"

"Do whatever you wish," I said. "My body is yours. Use it. Lick it. Fuck it. Whatever your heart desires. It isn't often that a man gets to have his way with a future king."

"I hope I don't disappoint."

"Never," I assured him. I grasped his cock and tugged on it. "Just go slowly. You are the first to be inside me, and I fear with the giant oak that is planted on you I'll never walk or sit again."

"I would never hurt you," he said. He kissed the palm of my hand before spitting into his own hand and slathering it onto his shaft and my waiting hole.

Tymon rested my ankles onto his shoulders, and with a delicate gentleness he used when crafting his spells, he held himself against my hole and pressed forward. Surprisingly, I opened for him, my anticipation obviously readying me.

"I've never wanted anyone the way I want you now," I said.

"I can tell." He inched forward, beyond the ring. We both gasped when he slid completely into me.

"By the gods, you're huge!" I shouted. "Don't stop. I can take it. Just fuck me. Fuck your king," I commanded.

He obliged. I felt heat building inside him, emanating into me through his cock, his shoulders, and his hands. He held nothing back, thrusting into me like a great siege engine built by an evil genius. My hole stretched to accommodate him, and Tymon fucked me with abandon. In and out, over and over, slamming every inch of his lovely, engorged mage's wand into my royal cavern.

Like Tymon, I never wanted this to end. "Hold—hold—hold it inside me," I panted.

He thrust all the way in, buried to his balls, pinning me to the mattress. My hulking farm hand-cum-mage obliged my every royal decree.

"Cum in me," I commanded.

He withdrew and renewed his thrusting. Within moments he screamed, "My prince!" and his balls unleashed a tidal wave of warmth. I felt it leaking around his cock and running down my back.

Tymon didn't stop until I was begging for him to withdraw.

"Did I hurt you?" he asked. He was instantly beside me, his slowly softening member resting on my shoulder.

I shook my head and ran a hand through his sopping wet hair. "I am not hurt. I just couldn't take another assault. You win. From now on, you can fuck me to your heart's content."

He kissed me passionately. "Let's clean up and grab refreshment. I believe I can go again before we sleep."

"As you command, my mage."

Chapter Five

For weeks, when Tymon could slip away after his studies, we found ourselves in my rooms. We most often barely made it to the bed before Tymon was fucking me. Finally, I had to have a plush rug installed to save my knees or back from the harsh, biting edges of the stones of my floor.

I don't know when things began to change, but it happened slowly. Tymon fell in love with me, but I came to see our trysts as a distraction, a dalliance of a young prince, sowing his royal seed in fertile pasture.

After several months, I tired of Tymon and refused to see him. Notes found their way to my chambers, and I returned simple missives that expressed my desire to move on. Eventually I no longer heard from Tymon, although an occasional black rose would await me on my pillow at night.

I cast them back into the shadows that had spawned them.

By winter solstice an up-and-coming knight, Sir Jullain of Fallnagard, had caught my eye. He was a fair, handsome man of thirty-some years, who had pledged fealty to my father when his own kingdom fell.

Jullain became my personal guard, and I immediately set about seducing him. It was a wonderful game because he was a stoic and dutiful man who prided himself on being a stalwart shield between me and those who would do me harm.

One night, I called him to my chambers. I wore a long robe that I'd loosely belted at my waist. My chest I left exposed, and having taken up more exercises with knights in the yards, I'd added a significant amount of muscle. Surely that would please and tempt my dear Jullain.

When he entered my rooms, I waited beside the massive stone fireplace, allowing the flickering flames to cast dancing shadows over me.

"You wished to see me, Your Highness?" Without looking I knew that he had fallen to one knee behind me. No matter how much I requested otherwise, he always kneeled before addressing me.

I turned, allowing the robe to catch on a stone and pull open enough to expose more of my chest. Against hope, his eyes never lifted.

"Rise, Jullain. Honestly, this constant need to remind you of my wishes becomes tiresome." I sounded petulant, and I knew it was because I was angry he wasn't taking the bait I had so meticulously prepared for him.

He stood immediately. "I'm sorry to have displeased you, my prince. Would you like to have me reassigned or punished? I can report to the king at once."

"No!" I shouted. I stalked across the room to him. My fury grew with every step, and when I came to a halt before him, my urge to strike him was overwhelming. "I don't want you reassigned or punished, damn it! I want you to fuck me!"

I clamped my lips shut, cursing myself for a fool. I felt the heat of embarrassment color my face, and I turned away. However, I saw the look in Jullain's eyes, and it scared and confused me.

"Get out," I commanded.

"My prince—"

"I said get out!" I whirled around, my fist flying through the air.

Jullain surprised me by catching my fist in the palm of his hand. He held it there, breathing like a stag running from the hunt, before he released me and fell to his knees.

"I beg pardon, my prince. I didn't mean to touch you."

Grasping his chin, I forced him to look at me. "Don't you understand? I *want* you to touch me. I've wanted nothing else since I first saw you."

"I know," he whispered.

I was stunned. "You know? Then why haven't you done anything about it?"

He suddenly wrapped his arms around my waist and pulled me to him, resting his head on my barely concealed cock. "I feared I wouldn't be able to protect you if I fell in love with you. I resisted because I didn't want to chance causing you harm through hesitation or inaction."

I undid the belt, and allowed the robe to slip from my shoulders. Jullain suddenly found himself holding onto a heap of fabric which he dropped. I felt the heat of his breath on my erection for several torturous seconds before he kissed it once.

"I will do as you command, my prince. You have but to give me orders. I'm yours," he said.

"I want you to fuck me," I said again.

"Then I will fuck you." He stood and scooped me into his arms. His stubbly beard grated against my smooth face as he smothered my mouth with a kiss.

He carried me to my bed and placed me gently upon the coverlet. I watched as he slowly undressed himself while never breaking eye contact. My cock hardened as more of his flesh came into view.

The most arousing aspect of Jullain's body was the myriad scars that crisscrossed his arms, chest, and stomach. The victor of many wars and skirmishes, his reputation was hard-won. Fully naked, he stood before me, taking his shaft in hand, making it battle-ready.

I pulled my knees to my chest. "I want you to fuck me with as much abandon as you would a tavern wench when celebrating a victory. Abuse my hole, Sir Jullain. Spill your seed in my guts the way you would spill blood upon the ground. I am your spoils. You must claim me."

I knew what I wanted, but I'd no idea that Jullain would take it so forcefully. He spat on his cock once, dragged me to the edge of the bed, and pushed into me without warning or preparation. I screamed then bit down on his well-calloused fingers when he forced them into my mouth.

A haze of lust and ownership passed over Jullain's eyes, and he did exactly as I commanded. He thrust into me over and over. The pain was excruciating, but I had never been harder. My desire to be possessed had never been as sharp.

In my mind I begged him to hurry, to fill me and then depart, leaving me a used whore in my own bed. It became obvious he had no such intentions. Jullain was undoubtedly well-versed in the strategies of sex, and his campaign had only just begun.

When he tired of standing, he fucked me farther toward the center of the bed and crushed me beneath the bulk of his warrior's body.

"Is this what you wanted, whelp?" he demanded. "You enjoy having this cock in you? You enjoy being fucked like daddy's little girl in the hayloft, do you? Well, I'll make you wish you had never hinted at wanting me in this sweet ass of yours. I'm going to fuck you until you die!"

I feared he truly meant it. If he did, I never found out.

Jullain's animalistic grunts were drowned out by an ear-shattering pop and the rush of air. Having spent so much time with Tymon, I knew the signs of a teleportation spell. The room suddenly began to fill with a thick, black mist, and Tymon stepped from the shadows at the foot of my bed.

Jullain saw him too, but for some reason he couldn't stop fucking me. I could see the struggle within him. "Release me, mage!"

Tymon ignored him. He stared sadly at me and tossed a single black rose onto the bed beside me. "This is why you no longer wish to see me? I've been cast aside for a brute who you've begged to rape you?"

I wanted him to scream the words, but they were said in a soft tone that immediately pierced my heart. When I tried to speak, Tymon flicked his hand, and Jullain's fingers filled my mouth again.

"I love you, Ruldaan," Tymon said. "I gave myself to you. I thought I meant something to you. Instead, I see that you're nothing but a common whore who wants to be fucked by every rough, unrefined dick that catches your eye."

I shook my head, gagging on Jullain's fingers in my attempts to speak. Tears flooded from my eyes. Jullain continued to fuck me with abandon. Without warning, he shot his seed into me, yet he continued to fuck me. Tymon was in control, and nothing could stop him.

"Since you have no concern for me or the damage you've done to my heart, I'll make you pay the price as long as you live." Tymon cast his hands to the side, and the mist began to swirl around him. Slowly it took on the form of a nightmare creature with a skull face and jagged, bat-like wings.

At a gesture, it flew to Jullain, latching onto his back. The knight screamed, and the mist entered through his mouth, choking him. Finally, free of Tymon's grasp, Jullain fell to the floor, writhing while the mist flowed from his mouth, nose, ears, and cock.

When he shuddered and lay still, the mist slithered up the side of the bed and across the coverlet. I attempted to thrash about and flee, but Tymon held me in his magical grip. I watched in horror as the mist flowed inside my battered hole.

I awaited death.

"From this day forward," Tymon said, "you condemn to death any man stupid enough to fall for your charms. Should any man fuck you or be fucked by you, the shadow assassin will murder him before your eyes. You'll have the rest of your life to ponder what you have done to me."

∞

Great sobs wracked my body as the full story came out. I still felt the pain I'd caused Tymon, and I still regretted it.

"After his proclamation, he disappeared. I couldn't apologize—not that it would have done any good. The damage was done." I stared down at Kradyn, seeing him through my tears. I was ashamed, but Kradyn looked on me with compassion in his eyes instead of the condemnation I deserved. "Now you know. That's why I had to stop you on the ship. If I hadn't, you'd be dead."

He stared up at me in quiet contemplation. He finally stood, and I feared that he would leave me standing alone in the midst of Genev's garden. However, he took me in his arms, pulled me close to him, and allowed me to cry into his shoulder. His hand stroked my hair and patted me on the back.

"You must leave me, Kradyn," I said when my tears finally stopped flowing. "I can never allow you to truly love me, neither physically nor spiritually. Either way will mean your death."

"Frankly, Ruldaan," he said, pulling me tighter to him, "that's not your decision to make. Let the damn sorcerer and his assassin come. They'll find me more than ample to the task of kicking both their asses."

I shook my head, and he covered my mouth with his own to stifle further arguments. I hated the desire I felt for him. I hated how he made me feel. Most of all I hated that I could never have him in me, even though I realized that I wanted him, not out of lust, but from a sense of love forming between us.

"No more tears," Kradyn commanded. "No more talk of shadow assassins or death. What's done is in the past. We must look forward to the future. I know we've only just met, but I love you. I won't let some mage stop that, no matter how broken and twisted his heart is."

I dried my tears and resolved to put aside my emotion where Tymon was concerned. It was one thing for Kradyn to see me so vulnerable, but it wouldn't do to have anyone from the royal court see me in such a state.

I'd made my decisions those years ago, and now I must deal with the consequences. I'd crushed Tymon's heart and soul, and now I was paying for those actions.

I looked into Kradyn's eyes, feeling the calling of the deepest oceans as the azure blue filled my soul with peace and calm. Kradyn never broke my gaze. I felt the passion radiating from him. His lust and desire to possess me. My heart pounded in my chest at the thought of having him take me there, in the gardens, for all to see. As our lips met in a tender kiss, Kradyn grabbed my ass with his powerful hands, crushing the flesh within his palms and pulling me to him.

Over and over in my mind I screamed, *You can't do this. You can't do this. It'll mean his death.* I recalled Kradyn's words, "Let the damn sorcerer and his assassin come."

But I couldn't allow that.

I pulled my lips from his and opened my eyes. "We can't, Kradyn. No matter how much I want to, we can't. I won't have you dead at my feet...like Jullain."

He smiled and gently brushed our lips together. "There will come a day when this bastard sorcerer has been annihilated, the curses from both you and your sister have been lifted, and when I shall have you for my own. And I *will* have you, Ruldaan. Every inch of me, filling every inch of you. Until you scream for release and mercy."

The intensity in his eyes and in his words mixed with a power I'd never felt from him before. As they poured from his lips with such determination and certainty, they tore a groan from my throat, and I felt my cock spasm with the thought of this giant man filling me with his seed and subjugating me to his will. I filled my breeches with cum, shuddering in Kradyn's arms as the orgasm shook my very core.

"That's only the beginning," he promised.

Chapter Six

"**W**hat became of the spell the Grand Magus gave you?" Kradyn asked. He sat with his leg draped over a sturdy wooden chair in my quarters aboard my ship. "It would seem he did a piss-poor job with the spell if it wouldn't protect you from Tymon's shadow assassin spell."

Reaching into my tunic, I removed a golden cylinder attached to a thick, rope-like chain around my neck and presented it to him. "I still have it. When I spoke to the Magus about my own similar thoughts, he told me the true need for it would present itself one day."

"I'd say the need presented itself when a shadow creature decided to take up residence in your ass." Kradyn coughed and cast me an apologetic sideways glance. "Well, that didn't come out the way I expected, but I'm sure you understand my meaning."

I chuckled and kissed him on top of his head. "I did. Although, I'll admit that sometimes you puzzle me. One minute you're talking like a scholar, and the next you're talking like a deckhand. You're an enigma."

He rubbed my back tenderly, intentionally—I'm sure—including the top of my ass in his attentions. Kradyn certainly enjoyed testing the limits of my resolve. I unscrewed the cap from the cylinder, shook out the rolled piece of scrollwork, and handed it to him. Using both hands, he unrolled it and scanned the page.

"Can you read it?" I asked after several minutes.

"Yes, but that doesn't mean it makes sense. Do you see the words here, here, and here?" He pointed where he wanted me to look. "Those are draconic words of great power."

"What do they mean?" I asked.

"That's the thing with draconic—it doesn't mean anything until you know the context of the conversation," he said. "A discussion between dragons can take a year just to get through the formal introductions. Then you have to take into consideration the motivations of each party, the time of year, who is in whose territory. There are so many criteria to know and understand."

"So the scroll is just gibberish?" I asked.

He contemplated the words on the paper again. "I don't believe so. I believe that Grand Magus of yours was a crafty man, who knew how to write spells that no one else could duplicate." He returned the scroll to me. "Even though I can't decipher the spell, I know that it's powerful. That mage is to be feared."

"He died several years ago," I said while tucking the metal cylinder back into my tunic.

"It may be for the best, as bad as it sounds," he said. "If he ever put his mind to it, he could have been a formidable foe."

"Dealing with one rogue mage is enough," I said.

"There's a difference between lashing out from hurt and being truly evil," Kradyn said. "I don't think Tymon is truly evil."

"Even taking into account the fact he murdered Jullain and has placed a curse on Genev and me?" I hadn't meant to put as much heat and hurt into my words, but it sounded to me like he was defending Tymon."

He pulled me onto his lap and pressed a finger to my lips. "Don't put words into my mouth. You know that's not what I meant," he said. "It's time for you to face the fact that you wounded Tymon in a way no one else could. You were his first, and from the sounds of it, what a first! We just need to hope that we can either get him to see reason or that we can kill him before he kills us."

"And to get the counterspell," I said. I suddenly realized how good it felt to be draped across Kradyn. While I wasn't a small man by any means, the size of him gave me great comfort and washed away all concerns.

"A counter-spell may not be necessary. When most mages die, their magic dies with them, unless it was written on paper, like your scroll," Kradyn said.

"So there's hope," I said.

"Well, not to sound cliche, but there is always hope," he said. "We just have to stay strong and determined. You can't give up or give in to despair, even if things appear bleak. I'm at your side, and I'll see you through this. Never forget that."

I rested my head on his shoulder and wrapped my arms around him. The prickling of his ever-present stubble on my cheek gave comfort, too. "I can never thank you enough for all you're doing for me and my family."

"Your thanks are not necessary," he said. "I do this because I want to, and because you need someone to help you. Besides, we might dig a fairytale ending out of this muck."

"Where we live happily ever after?" I asked with a wry smile.

"That, and where I get to bury my cock in your ass and hear you beg for mercy," he said. He slammed his crotch into my ass a couple times, laughing and kissing me in turn.

I stood up abruptly and rushed to the door.

"What's wrong?" he asked.

"I need to take some air before I give in to you and we both regret it," I said.

"I would die with no regrets," he said. I saw the seriousness in his eyes.

"Well of course you wouldn't have regrets," I said. "You would die after having the hottest ass in the kingdom wrapped snugly around your cock. Who wouldn't want that?"

I smiled broadly and left Kradyn in the cabin alone with his raucous laughter.

∞

"The High Wizard of the Full Moon believes that's where Tymon is hiding?" First Mate Biddon asked. He had unrolled a map on a table aft of the wheel. The area he indicated was a marsh with no name.

"Yes, that's what he said according to Rofek," I said. "By my calculations, we should arrive early tomorrow morning."

"Agreed."

"What's troubling you?" Having known Biddon most of my life, I could tell there was something preoccupying him, some concern he wasn't voicing.

"Do you believe we can trust the dragon?" he asked.

"Kradyn trusts him. For me, that's enough," I said. "The bigger question is do *you* trust the dragon?"

Biddon rolled up the map and stowed it in a hard-leather tube he stoppered and placed in a crate with similar devices. "I honestly don't see what choice we have. Bronzes aren't known for being evil or deceptive." He took a deep breath and leaned on the table, staring at me. "I'm just concerned about your safety and healing Princess Genev."

I clapped him on the back. "You're a true friend, Biddon, and I appreciate your concern. I trust you to be watchful and wary, of everything and everyone. Your instincts and insights have never failed me."

Biddon bowed slightly—something he never did onboard—and relieved the sailor at the wheel. He shouted orders to some sailors lollygagging on the maindeck. Cries from the crow's nest caught his attention and mine, and a sailor ran to us from the main mast.

"There's a storm sighted port, Captain," the man said to me.

I retrieved a spyglass from Biddon's effects and scanned the horizon. "It's moving this way very quickly." My breath caught in my throat when a massive bolt of lightning arced out from the roiling black mass of clouds and struck the water relatively close to the vessel. "This isn't a natural storm."

The air *popped* and *whooshed*, and I turned to find Arvon wobbling on the deck in an attempt to get his sea legs after teleporting aboard. He was out of breath and looked on the verge of losing his breakfast on the deck. I helped steady him.

"Your Majesty, you're in grave danger," he said through his ragged attempts at pulling air into his lungs. He looked at the horizon and turned pale. "I'm too late."

All the men on deck shouted and ran for cover when another bolt of lightning—followed by an immediate peal of thunder—struck the side of the ship. The storm was upon us, when only moments before it had been miles away.

Flames reached skyward from the bow, and sailors raced with buckets to douse them. However, the more water thrown into the growing conflagration, the more it fed and spread.

"It's mage fire," Arvon said. "I'll see to it. You should prepare to abandon ship, Ruldaan." He raced away without bothering with my protestations.

"What the hell is going on?" Kradyn lurched through the door of my cabin when a massive wave struck the ship.

Two men fell overboard. Looking along the side of the ship, I didn't see them for several seconds, but finally their heads surfaced. Someone threw them a line, but the swell threatened to swallow them again.

Chaos spread like the mage's fire. Arvon had convinced most of the sailors to abandon their firefighting efforts and was concentrating his spells on the purplish-orange flames. I knew without a doubt that his efforts were in vain, and I'm sure he knew it, too, but that didn't hinder him.

"Biddon, it's time to abandon ship," I ordered before jumping over the rail to the deck below. Kradyn steadied me when I landed because the previously level surface suddenly shifted due to a massive wave. It wasn't exactly the smartest thing I could've done.

"We won't stand a chance in life boats," Kradyn said.

"It's either that or be cooked by mage fire." I watched Arvon fall back as a giant wall of flame suddenly roared over the rail. He threw up a defensive spell that saved him from being consumed, but just barely. "We have no options," I said.

A bolt of lightning struck the mainsail, setting it ablaze. Smoldering, burning pieces of canvas rained down, adding to the general melee. Kradyn shoved me aside as a splintered beam fell where I'd been standing moments before.

"Abandon ship!" I shouted once I was on my feet again.

Even before my command, men had started preparations to deploy the craft. Biddon left the wheel, allowing the ship to go where the storm sent it, and he joined in helping his men.

A sailor leaning on the rail screamed moments before a monstrous wave washed over the ship. He and several others slid across the deck, caught in the rushing, foamy fury, and disappeared over the side not a few feet from where I stood. The sea swallowed them, and they didn't reemerge.

"It's time to get you out of here," Kradyn said.

"I won't leave my men."

"You're a king, and your first duty is to live so you can rule your people." Kradyn grabbed hold of me and ushered me toward the nearest boat. "Get in, or I'll put you in."

"Fine, but you come with me." I saw him hesitate and look over his shoulder. "If you don't go, I don't go."

"Damn it, Ruldaan," he grumbled, but he got into the boat with me.

The small craft hit the churning surface of the ocean, the ropes were cast aside, and men rowed away from the ship. I watched helplessly as my subjects fought valiantly to get to safety themselves. They were sworn to protect me with their lives, but that didn't make it easier for me to accept.

"Brace yourselves!"

The warning came too late. A rogue wave slammed into the boat, and I went into the water. I struggled to reach the surface again, but the swirling waters dragged me farther down.

Just when my strength began to wane, and my lungs were on the verge of forcing me to inhale, a massive darkness rose from the depths. I lost consciousness moments before I saw what it was.

Chapter Seven

*T*he sound of surf in my ears, and the grit of sand in my teeth greeted me when I opened my eyes. The sun beat down on me without mercy. I spit, coughed, spit again, and rolled onto my back.

"Are you well, Your Majesty?"

My head lolled to the side, and I saw Biddon staring at me from his own prone position in the sand a few feet away. Groaning, I sat up and looked around before saying, "I believe so. Are you?"

He shook his head. "I believe my leg's broken. As long as I don't move, I'm mostly fine, but the pain is excruciating."

I rushed to his side and inspected the leg he indicated. Thankfully the bone was still beneath the skin, but I could clearly see it was badly broken and would require extensive care to mend. Unfortunately, I found myself alone with Biddon, and help was hundreds of miles away.

A great roar sounded in the distance. I realized we were at the edge of the swampy marshlands where Tymon lived. Birds flew in all directions from tall trees that stood on roots slightly elevated from the ground. Great strands of moss hung like garland, and in the more dark recesses of the thickening forest, fairy lights danced briefly.

The hair on my neck and arms rose when the roar repeated itself. I searched frantically for something to defend us, but I wasn't in the habit of carrying a sword, and Biddon and I were lucky just to have the tattered remnants of our clothes to protect our modesty.

"You must leave me, Your Majesty," he told me.

"You know that isn't going to happen," I said.

"But—"

"I won't hear any more about it. Now, I'm sorry, but we have to move you. I don't know what manner of creature that is, but given the noise and the fact we're near a swamp, my bet is on black dragon." I sat him up and pointedly ignored the fact he soiled himself in the process.

"Gods!" he screamed. His breaths came in rapid pants, and I feared he would pass out.

"You can do this, Biddon. Lean on me. I'll help you, but we must move." I struggled with him as he rose, but finally we both had our feet beneath us. "Good man. Now comes the hard part."

We took one step and promptly fell on our faces. The ground beneath us began to vibrate, and I could see it ripple into the water when the waves washed out. As the tremors intensified, I knew the beast was heading our way.

"Get up," I commanded.

"Leave me," Biddon cried. "The pain is too much. Go, before you're killed."

"I said get up!"

Biddon pushed me away. His shock at having treated his king in such a way passed quickly. "Go, please. I won't be responsible for your death."

"Damn it." I ignored his further pleas for me to flee and placed myself between him and the tree line. There was no doubt we'd both be mercilessly rent to pieces in the jaws of whatever creature had caught our scent, but I refused to use Biddon as bait just to save myself.

Another roar from overhead caught my attention, and a greenish-gold blur streaked through the air and crashed into the trees. A great cacophony of animal sounds, crashing trees, and fleeing birds became almost deafening. I couldn't move because I was so transfixed by the unseen titanic battle.

Biddon had ceased urging me to flee, and I realized he had passed out. At least that would give him respite from pain and relieve him of seeing the end come in a gnashing of teeth.

In the distance the battle raged on, but if I wasn't mistaken, the sounds were getting more distant. I exhaled a held breath and tried to focus on a plan to help Biddon.

"Ruldaan!"

"Kradyn, thank the gods." I ran to him as he emerged from the trees. I fell into his outstretched arms and smothered his mouth with frantic kisses.

"Are you injured?" he asked.

"No, but Biddon's leg is badly broken. Can you help me carry him?"

"Yes, but we must hurry," he said. "Rofek has another dragon on the run, but I don't know how long he can hold out."

"We should help him." I realized the stupidity of my words as soon as they left my mouth, but it was too late. Thankfully Kradyn ignored them and focused on Biddon.

With no sign of effort or strain, he scooped the brawny first mate from the sand and began running along the beach. "There's a cave not far from here. It's small enough the black can't enter if he gets away from Rofek and comes for us."

Even with him carrying such a heavy burden, I was hard pressed to keep pace with Kradyn. He was a tireless machine who churned through the sand like he was running on air carrying nothing at all. I marveled at his strength.

In the distance, still moving away from the beach, the black gave a short, angry roar. Rofek followed with a triumphant bellow, and then silence reigned. I saw the cave ahead, and thanked the gods for it. My legs and lungs burned with an unseen fire I thought would consume me.

Inside the cave—which was rather boring as far as caves go—Kradyn gently placed Biddon on the floor. "This leg is going to need an expert healer," he said.

"I know." I stood over him as he ran his hand over the first mate's leg. "I wish we could get him back to Nwansk."

"With Rofek's help that may be possible," Kradyn said.

"What happened to Arvon and the others?" I asked.

"I don't know. When our boat capsized, I lost track of everyone." Kradyn abandoned his examination and sat back, absentmindedly running his hand up and down my thigh. "I don't know how I made it to shore, but when I woke up, I began exploring."

"And found a black dragon," I said.

"I'm just lucky that way." He chuckled and pulled me down beside him, embracing and kissing me. "I'm glad you're safe. I'd feared the worst."

"As did I." I kissed him again.

A rush of wind and a growl from the cave entrance preceded Rofek, who landed and poked his head inside. "You're safe?" he asked.

Kradyn hurried to the dragon and began checking him over. "We are. What about you?"

Rofek made a horrible noise that I finally determined was the dragon equivalent of laughter. "I'm young and agile. The black is old, fat, and too sure of himself. There was never any doubt in my mind who would be victorious."

"Ah, the arrogance of youth," Kradyn said. He patted Rofek's head. "Thank you for coming to my aid."

Rofek glanced at me briefly. "You're welcome."

I could have sworn I heard him mutter, "Not that you needed help."

"Did the High Wizard have what I requested?" Kradyn asked when he was apparently sure his friend wasn't injured.

Rofek closed his eyes and began humming deep within his throat. After a few seconds he said a few words in draconic that forced me to clamp my hands to my ears. Momentarily, what looked like a bullseye lantern materialized in front of him, suspended in mid-air.

Kradyn took hold of it. "Thank you."

"The price is high," Rofek warned. "The wizard said you would know what was required."

"It's worth it," Kradyn said.

Rofek glanced at me again. "I certainly hope so."

Kradyn cleared his throat. "I have another task for you, if you're willing. This human is injured," he said, pointing to Biddon. "He needs to be returned to Nwansk to a healer. Would you fly him there?"

Rofek sighed and shook from his nose to the tip of his tail. "Fine, but afterward I'm returning to the cave to rest. Oh, and I'm eating those two black pearls you've been admiring when you think I'm not looking."

Kradyn scowled. "You and wizards. Between the two of you, you'll bleed me dry and eat me out of house and home. Very well, just be gentle with him."

I offered to help place Biddon on Rofek's back, but Kradyn took care of it with no effort. He hugged Rofek and bid him safe journey, and then the dragon was gone.

Kradyn sat down beside me again, turning the lantern over and over in his hands. He scrutinized the object in silence, and while I wanted to ask, I knew he would tell me in due time.

"I have a way we can locate Tymon," he said finally.

"Using a lantern?" I asked.

He set it on the ground between his legs and took my hand in his. I could feel the steady thrumming of his heart, and the warmth of his hands warmed my body like lava warms the ground. I scooted closer to him, enjoying the sensation and the feelings proximity stirred within me.

"It looks like a lantern, but it's not," he said. "It's actually a spirit trap. They're very rare because they're so hard to construct. It takes a skilled mage who has spent a lifetime practicing magic. Even then it can be a deadly undertaking."

"What's it used for, and how will it help us?" I wasn't making the connection between the cage and our need to locate Tymon.

"The cage is used—as the name implies—to trap a spirit within its confines. Once inside, the spirit must do the bidding of whoever possesses the trap." He stared intently into my eyes and grasped my hands. "I want to use it to trap the shadow assassin and force him to lead us to Tymon."

"Is that possible?" I asked.

"It is, but there's no guarantee that it'll work," he said. "Any of a number of things could go wrong, including both of us dying."

"If we don't find Tymon, then Genev will certainly die. It sounds like this is our only hope. What do we have to do?" I asked.

"I need to exorcise the shadow from you," Kradyn said.

"How?" I asked. I suddenly didn't like where this was going.

"The easiest way is the best way." He smiled at me, and it was full of uncertainty and desire that set my heart racing. "Let me make love to you."

Chapter Eight

"What? No! Absolutely not!" I jerked my hands free and stood up. Kradyn attempted to grab me, but I evaded his grasp and marched outside.

He was beside me within seconds. "Ruldaan, stop and listen."

"I'm not listening because the plan is insane. I'm not doing it," I said. "Think of something else."

"There isn't anything else, damn it." He wrapped both his arms around my waist and bodily restrained me from taking another step. "Now stop, shut up, and listen to me."

The hair all over my body stood on end because of the desire to run from his fury. I thought about struggling to break free again, but I didn't want to test the limits of his love for me. Not that I thought he would hurt me—I never feared that. He just had that determined sound in his voice I knew I couldn't reason with.

"This is crazy. You'll die," I said. I relaxed and leaned back against him, my head on his shoulder.

"Possibly. If we don't find Tymon, Genev will die. Besides, do you really want to go through the rest of your life without any form of physical intimacy?" he asked.

"This isn't about me. This is about you and Genev," I said. "I'm fine with paying the consequences for my treatment of Tymon. Nobody else should have to."

"First, Genev won't die. Second, this is my decision," he said.

"Well, unless you plan on raping me, I have a say in whether or not you do anything," I said. I turned in his arms and embraced him tightly. "I know you're right, but I can't bear the thought of you dying because of me."

"I don't plan on dying."

"Well, I didn't plan on having a vengeful sorcerer fill my ass with a spirit, remember? I think we've covered that." I hated the heat in my voice, but the fearful thought of losing him was making me angry.

"We have to try." His tone left no place for further argument.

I gave in like he knew I would. "Fine. But, I don't want this to just be a quick fuck. If we're going to do this for what may be our only time, I want it to mean something."

"How long do we have before the assassin manifests?" he asked.

"I don't know," I said. "Since Jullain, I've not been with another man. It could be as soon as we start doing more than you jerking me off, or it could be as soon as you're in me. I don't know the rules."

"Then I suppose we'll find out." He forced me to look up at him and kissed me softly. "Let's go back inside. I promise I'll make it a memorable experience, especially if it's the last."

"Stop saying that," I ordered.

"Very well." He released me and led me back to the cave.

"Not a very romantic place," I said. The cave was all sand, stone, and rough edges that did nothing to put me in the mood for love making. Thankfully, I had Kradyn—the great beast of a man who had been chomping at the bit to impale me on his cock—to fill that role.

"It's not a pile of gold coins, that's for sure," he said. "I think we can use our clothes to cover that large, flat rock over there. It's not a king's bed, but it beats having sand in sensitive spots."

"Says the man who'll be doing his best to drive me through that rock," I said.

"I doubt I'll get that carried away." He winked at me.

"No, wait," I said when he started undoing the ties of his shirt. "Special, remember? Don't just strip off and rut."

"Right. Sorry. I'm just so eager to finally be with you."

I tossed the spirit trap to him. "Do you need this close by?"

"Probably." He placed it close to the stone wall and turned back to me. "Ready?"

"What choice do I have?" I sighed and walked around him to sit on the rock. "In case I don't get the chance to say this in a better time and place, I love you. I know it's sudden, and Mother would be apoplectic to hear me say it, but it's true."

"I love you, too. Now relax and prepare yourself for something amazing." He growled the last word, and my cock stirred.

I leaned back, supporting myself on one arm while I slowly rubbed myself with the opposite hand. Kradyn stared down at me for several seconds before he smoothly ran both his hands up from his stomach to his chest.

The ties from his shirt came undone in fingers that I knew were strong and gentle. They dangled momentarily before he reached a hand inside and tweaked one of his nipples. He sighed and licked his lips, never breaking eye contact with me.

Achingly slowly, he pulled the shirt over his head and tossed it aside. I'd never seen his bare chest, and the sight of it took my breath away. Firm muscles were covered with a dusting of hair as black as that on his head. He flexed for me, grinning at the moans it elicited.

"You like what you see?"

"Very much so," I said. I moved to free my erection from its painful prison.

"Uh uh. Leave it," Kradyn commanded.

I groaned but complied with his request, having to content myself with rubbing my engorged cock through the ocean-ravaged fabric. There was no telling how long I could hold out, but something told me that Kradyn wouldn't let me stop with just climaxing once. He'd waited for this moment, and I could tell he intended to indulge his desires for as long as it suited him.

Kradyn continued to run his hands over the taut, bulging firmness of his chest and torso. He tweaked a nipple with one hand while rubbing the palm of his other hand over the growing mountain in his pants. I'm sure I was mistaken, but I could have sworn I heard stitches popping.

Finally—by the gods, finally!—he undid the bindings of the breeches and began tugging them down. He turned his back to me, and I watched the tantalizing mounds of his ass peaking out at me. Slowly. Inch by inch the twin globes surfaced until, at last, I beheld his magnificent ass like a pilgrim beholding a holy site for the first time.

Now, I just had to look upon the face of a god, and life would be complete.

He smacked his ass—hard—leaving behind a hand print that quickly faded before being replaced with another. By the time his pants hit the sandy cave floor, both cheeks were rosy. I wanted to kiss away the pain—hell, I wanted to explore his ass like none other before.

It took me a moment to realize that Kradyn had turned around because I was so lost in the fantasy of his ass. Both of his massive hands were held in front of his crotch, obviously restraining his cock. He came closer, standing above me. His eyes were filled with a burning hunger I intended to sate.

He kneeled down, resting his knees on the rock bed beside me. I looked back and forth between his ravenous eyes and the hidden treasure. Nothing could prepare me for its unveiling.

One hand moved from his crotch to mine, thrusting past the waist to roughly wrap around my shaft. Kradyn squeezed and tugged it, driving me closer to the edge.

"Don't cum." The command was so forceful I almost came from the sheer power of the words. "You cum only when I tell you to."

I licked my lips. "If you keep that up, I can't make promises."

"Don't. Cum." He withdrew his hand, pulling my cock upward until it peaked from my trousers. His fingers played in circles over the head, smearing copious amounts of precum. He licked his fingers clean and moaned.

I ran my hands over his stomach, resisting the nearly overwhelming urge to tear his hand away from his groin so I could see what he was hiding from me. The contact of my flesh on his was almost electric.

By the time I realized he freed his cock, it was resting against my mouth. Kradyn painted my lips with his precum, rubbing the tip back and forth. I licked them clean then swabbed the head. It was massive! I suddenly felt a tingling fear unlike anything I'd ever experienced. I wanted the behemoth inside me, but I feared I would be destroyed by the experience.

"By the gods, it's so big." I stared in hungry fascination.

Kradyn gently slapped my face with it, and I felt the weight and girth of it. "Can you handle it?"

"Let's just say that if the shadow assassin doesn't kill me, I'm certain you will." I opened my mouth as wide as I could and pulled the head inside. More precum covered my tongue, and I savored the tangy sweetness. I wanted all of him inside me, but there was no way to get more than a few inches into my mouth.

"Don't hurt yourself," Kradyn said. He pulled back so he slipped from my mouth. He kissed me, and I let him taste himself.

He made quick work of undressing me, apparently not wanting to waste more time. My trousers had barely hit the cave floor when Kradyn had swallowed my cock. He swung a leg over my head so he was straddling me, and I took as much of him as I could into my mouth. The sensation of his hot breath on my ass had me squirming so I could expose more of it to him.

The sounds of frenzied slurping and sucking bounced from the rock walls, giving the sense of being in the midst of an insatiable orgy. Kradyn held nothing back. He was almost possessed of a demon the required sexual energy to live.

When my jaws became too sore to continue sucking, I forced him down lower, and my tongue found its way into the valley between his iron ass cheeks. His moans with me still in his mouth elicited a gasp from me. I spasmed.

"Don't cum," he commanded before swallowing me again.

I responded by forcing my tongue deeper into his trench, doing what I could to drive him insane. If he was set on torturing me, I would return the favor. Somehow, though, the odds still felt stacked in his favor.

Soon, Kradyn was splitting his attention between my cock and my own hole. He worked his spit into me along with several fingers. When he added his fourth finger I was beyond being able to reciprocate any attentions at all. He finally settled on rolling my legs and hips toward my chest, and he plundered my ass with abandon.

"Please, you've got to fuck me," I begged.

His tongue pressed past the ring of my sphincter, and when he pulled back, his fingers filled me. I willed myself into a state of relaxful bliss.

"I think you're ready." He stood up and pulled me to my feet. Before I could kiss him, he forced me back onto the stone slab on my knees facing away from him. "Bow to me, Your Majesty. It's time you surrender your most prized possession to my whims."

"I surrender," I said.

"Not yet, you haven't."

I felt him behind me, rubbing his shaft up and down the length of my crevice. It forced my cheeks apart and burned my hole with its heat. I quivered from anticipation, backing up against him. He slapped my ass. I moaned.

As quickly as I felt a glob of his spit dripping onto my eager hole, the head of his battering ram was at the gates. It demanded the surrender he had spoken of, and I gladly gave it.

"I'm yours, Kradyn. I pledge myself to you." He pressed the head against me in preparation for invasion. "If you die because of this, I'll find someone to resurrect you. And then I'll kill you again myself."

"I have the trap readied. Relax and enjoy me."

He pressed forward.

"Don't die, Kradyn." I couldn't help myself saying it.

He leaned down and kissed my neck. "I promise."

"Liar."

"I promise."

He whispered a few words I couldn't understand, but they washed over me like a blanket of cooling water. I sighed, and he pushed forward against my ass. When the head of his cock broke through my outer defenses, I groaned.

Kradyn stopped. "Get used to it. Let yourself—Oh gods! That feels amazing!"

I tightened and relaxed my muscles, massaging him while I slowly pushed backward. Kradyn wanted to be gentle, and while I definitely didn't want him to hurt me, I wanted so badly for him to fuck me that I couldn't wait.

Inch by inch I moved backward. Kradyn whispered unknown words the entire time. Briefly, I forgot about the shadow assassin until I felt Kradyn's body pressed up against mine. I stopped, waited.

"You feel amazing." Kradyn rubbed my ass cheeks and bumped into me several times without withdrawing. "Such a snug cave, it feels like home."

"Fuck me," I whispered. Then, more commanding, "Fuck me, Kradyn. Your king demands it."

"As you wish, Your Majesty."

I immediately felt empty as Kradyn withdrew all but the very tip of his cock and then slammed it back into me. Again and again he repeated the stroke until I thought I would lose consciousness from the air being forced from my lungs. He forced his way into places within me no other man had ever dreamed of reaching.

"Yes, Kradyn. Yes!" Without warning I felt cum explode from me. It splattered against the rock. I screamed, my muscles spasming and milking Kradyn's cock.

He screamed. And he screamed again, causing the hair on my body to stand on end. The animalistic shout didn't cease. My baser instincts took over, and I attempted to pull away from him, but he wrapped his arms around me to prevent my escape.

"No," he said.

Then I felt the volcanic eruption deep inside me. Kradyn lay atop me, forcing me down into the puddle of my own seed. Relentlessy he continued to fuck me, cumming the entire time. I thought it would never end, and soon felt warm rivers cascading over my balls.

Just as Kradyn grunted and thrust one last time, the cave was bathed in darkness, and an inhuman scream echoed from the walls. Kradyn withdrew from me.

"Come and get me," he said.

Chapter Nine

I rolled over onto my back. The smoky shadow assassin hung briefly in the air between Kradyn and me, and then it lashed out at him with blinding speed. Kradyn already had the spirit trap in hand. It glowed with an eerie greenish-blue light.

The spirit appeared unfazed by the magical contraption and engulfed Kradyn within its darkness. I attempted to stand but found myself inexplicably rooted in place.

"Kradyn!" I screamed and fought against the invisible force keeping me in place. "Fight it. You have to."

"What...do you think....I'm doing?" His voice sounded weak and strained.

Suddenly a massive clawed arm punched through the stygian mist and slashed at the assassin. The shadow shrieked. Green light exploded from the center of the scrum, and then a noise like a raging wind drowned out every other sound.

Within seconds the assassin disappeared, and the glowing trap fell to the ground, quickly followed by Kradyn. Finally I could move, and I rushed to him. His body was covered in thick, black goo. It oozed from the myriad wounds and claw marks crisscrossing his body.

Panic set in when I realized I couldn't do anything for him. Then, miraculously, the wounds sealed themselves shut, and Kradyn rolled onto his stomach.

"Kradyn! Kradyn, are you alright?" I ran my hands over his body, feeling for myself that he had been made whole. "How did you do that? Is it magic?"

"Yes," he groaned. He foreced himself up onto an elbow. The look in his eyes spoke of his exhaustion and determination. "I told you I wouldn't die."

I kissed him. Our bodies collided, and I sat atop him, frantically showering him with kisses and tears of happiness. "You scared the hell out of me. Why didn't you tell me you're a mage? I wouldn't have been so worried."

"Because I'm not a mage." He pushed me back and held me firmly by the shoulders. "I'm a dragon."

I laughed. "Right, of course you are." I laughed again and attempted to lean in for another kiss.

Kradyn restrained me. "I'm a dragon, Ruldaan. I'm the bronze dragon you sought. You met me in my cave. I saved you from drowning—twice—and I trapped the shadow assassin using dragon magic. I. Am. A. Dragon."

I sat staring down at him, more stunned than I'd ever been. "You don't look like a dragon."

He laughed. "I polymorphed myself into a human."

"Well, obviously you did." I felt stupid. "A dragon?" My body went numb, and when I felt his grip relax, I stood up.

"You're angry." Kradyn looked up at me, and I saw sadness and fear on his face—two emotions I never thought I would see there. "I didn't intend to deceive you."

I couldn't speak. What could I say? The words came suddenly and without thought. "But I love you. How can I love a dragon?"

I grabbed my clothes and walked woodenly from the cave. The sun overhead blinded me with its brilliance. Shading my eyes, I walked toward the waves, feeling the cooling breeze wash over me the way...Kradyn's words had. He'd used dragon magic on me. To relax me. So he could fuck me.

Anger welled up inside me, and I stopped and turned midstride. I slammed into Kradyn's chest and fell onto my bare ass in the sand. My anger intensified.

"You lied to me!" I shouted the words with such force my voice cracked. "You used me. I let you fuck me! Did I have any choice in the matter, or did you use dragon magic to bend my will?"

"I would never do that." Kradyn held his hand out to me, but I ignored it. He shrugged and stepped back a few paces. "Ruldaan, I love you. I genuinely love you, and I would never force you to do something you didn't want to do. Yes, I used my magic on you while we made love, but it was only to ease your pain and heighten your enjoyment. I feared losing control and hurting you. Your mere presence drives me mad with lust and desire."

"You're a dragon, Kradyn!"

"Would you stop saying that?" he asked. "I know what I am."

"How can a dragon love a human?" I asked.

"How can a human love another human?" he asked. "I do have a heart, you know."

"How—" By the gods, what was I to do? I wanted to throw myself at him and have him fuck me again, but I also had no idea how to reconcile the fact he was truly a massive creature of great power wrapped inside a magical facade. "I want to see your true form."

He sighed. "Will that make a difference?"

"I-I don't honestly know," I said. "But that is beside the point. I think I'm entitled to see who, what I just let inside me."

"I'm not a 'what.' I do have feelings, and you're treading on them very firmly," he said.

"I'm sorry." I stood up without his assistance. "I want to see your true form. Please, Kradyn."

"Very well." He turned around and walked away from me, back toward the cave. When he stopped, he faced me, gave me a sad smile, and began muttering words I shouldn't have been able to hear but did.

I expected a great display of magic—vivid lights, sparks, a cacophony of sounds—but instead I simply felt a rush of air, and then I found myself face to face with a bronze dragon—literally. Kradyn's face was mere inches from mine.

"By the gods." I felt his breath on my face, and it smelled of ocean salt and pearls. "You are magnificent."

Timidly, I reached out a hand and ran it over the greenish-gold scales of his snout. He turned his massive head to the side and looked at me with one eye.

"Are you afraid?" I'd expected his voice to be booming and overpowering, but, like his magic, it washed over me with comfort.

"No. Well, not entirely."

Slowly I moved from his snout and walked past his long neck, which was covered in scales and topped by bony plates. The claws on his feet were massive, almost as long as my forearm, and I knew they were powerful enough to fell many creatures at once.

I'd almost reached the cave before I was able to walk around the tip of his long, muscular tail and start my journey back to his face. There was no denying Kradyn was a magnificent beast. I just didn't know if I could come to terms with the fact he was really a dragon.

When I reached his head again, he unfolded his wings and spread them overhead. The sun was blocked completely, and I stood in cool shade.

"You are amazing," I said. "This is all so much to wrap my mind around."

Kradyn said a few indecipherable words, and then his human form stood naked before me. "I didn't intentionally deceive you. I just didn't know when to tell you, and then I suddenly found myself without an explanation when I survived the assassin."

With trepidation he extended his hand toward me and brushed my cheek. "I would never hurt you, Ruldaan. I didn't coerce you into loving me or making love to me. Please believe me."

"I do," I said. I grabbed his hand—which had been a massive, claw-lined foot a few moments before—and kissed the palm. "I was just so shocked by your confession and the truth. It's just overwhelming, but I think I can adjust."

"I am so happy to hear you say that." He smiled and pulled me into a tight embrace and breath-stealing kiss. When he released me, he said, "Now, let's put Tymon's creature to our own use and find him."

"First, I need to take care of something." I looked down at the dried cum and sand plastered all over my body. "You didn't exactly leave me in a clean state."

Kradyn laughed and scooped me into his arms. "By the gods, Ruldaan, that ass of yours *should* be a temple! I could worship at it for days."

He carried me toward the surf. Our lips pressed together as the first wave washed over our bodies.

Chapter Ten

"**I** still say it would be faster to fly," I said. Hanging moss brushed against my face before I could push it out of the way, and I stepped into another hole in the brackish water. "This is ridiculous. Why couldn't Tymon hide out somewhere more hospitable?"

Kradyn laughed. "Would you like me to summon a palanquin to carry Your Majesty through the swamp?"

"Transform and fly me," I said, hating the petulance and whining tone of my own voice.

"I told you, we risk the black's attention if I do that. He'll sense me in human form, but in my true form he'll be honor bound to treat me as a true threat to his territory," Kradyn said.

He stopped suddenly and swung the spirit trap to the left and then right before continuing straight ahead. "We'll be there soon enough. I can feel the wards the sorcerer has set."

"If there are wards then won't he know we're coming?" I asked.

"Maybe. I've been working my own magic on them, and I think I've been able to fool them," Kradyn said.

"You would be sadly mistaken."

"Tymon!" I whirled around just in time to catch a small globe of energy in the chest. It enveloped me and when Tymon retracted his hand, I flew to him.

"Come get me, dragon," Tymon said, and then we teleported away.

∞

The iron-bound wooden door slammed shut behind me before Tymon released his magical grip on me. I rushed back toward it, but the door refused to budge, no matter how violently I slammed into it. I don't know what I was expecting, but doing something, no matter how foolish, was better than doing nothing.

He slid aside a small piece of metal near the top of the door and peered in at me. "Save your strength, Ruldaan. You'll need it for when your pet gets here," he said. The ire dripping from his words could have cut through the stones of the floor.

"Why are you hurting Genev? I'm the one you're angry at. Kill me," I said.

"But I *am* killing you. I see how badly it is affecting you that I have cast the spell on your dear sister." His voice was full of joy. "Your mother will be next, once dear Genev succumbs to my magic. Then, we'll see what I can do to your dragon and the rest of your kingdom."

"I'm going to kill you," I said.

"You'll forgive me if I don't appear frightened by your words." Tymon slid the metal back into place. "Rest up. When the big lizard gets here, I'm going to murder him in front of you."

I slammed against the door one more time, and then slid to the floor. Something stabbed into my chest, and I angrily pulled the metal scroll case from my shirt.

Some use it was! Did I have to be knocking on death's door in order to for the stupid spell to work? So many appropriate situations had arisen, and not even a trickle of magic had made itself known.

"Don't worry yourself, Your Majesty. Kradyn will come for you."

I suddenly realized I wasn't alone. "Who is there? Rofek?"

From the shadows, a stooped figure shambled forward and squatted a few feet away. "Yes."

I moved closer and squinted to see in the shadowy darkness of the cell. "What happened to you?" His face was terribly misshapen, and his body was stunted and deformed. How he managed to move about was truly a miracle.

Rofek sighed. "The damned sorcerer forced me to polymorph, and he has cast a silence spell upon me to prevent me from using magic. He made me as hideous as possible."

I realized he was crying and pulled him to me, embracing and cradling him in my arms. "We're going to make this right. I promise."

Rofek held me tightly. "I'm sorry I was rude to you on your ship."

"Don't worry about it," I said. "Is Biddon safe? How did Tymon capture you, anyway? You should be in Nwansk."

"He's fine. I left him with a healer and then came back to help you and Kradyn," he said. "Unfortunately, Tymon found me before I found you."

All the air in the room felt like it had suddenly become very thick, almost gelatinous, and then Arvon stepped into existence in the center of the room.

"Well, that was nasty business." He brushed off his sleeves and turned to face us. "Your Majesty, I've come to rescue you."

"How were you able to teleport in here?" I asked.

"I had some help from the High Wizard," he said. "That's why the spell feels different. I almost didn't make it through the wards Tymon set. Thankfully he's not as all-powerful as he'd like to think."

"Take Rofek and go," I ordered.

"But, Your—"

"No, you have to do this," I said. "Kradyn is coming for me, and I won't leave him alone with Tymon. Take Rofek back to the High Wizard and dispel the magicks on him."

"I cannot in good conscience—"

"That's an order," I said.

Arvon sighed and shook his head. "With all due respect, Your Majesty, I hate it when you do that."

"I know." I shocked him by giving him a hug. "But I know you're loyal and will do as I ask. I wish I had a million more of you."

"I still wouldn't be able to get you to see sense," he muttered. "Come, Rofek, let's get you out of here."

They disappeared and I slid back onto the floor.

"That was so touching." The door opened and Tymon pointed at me.

My body spasmed, and then I was immobile again. He suspended me from the floor. "Why didn't you try to stop them?"

"My plans are my own," he said. "Come. We must make ready for the dragon."

∞

"Are you serious?" I stood naked before Tymon. He had stripped me of my clothes then manacled me to a beam in front of a massive throne. His attempts to remove the scroll tube from my neck had proven futile. It had burned him badly when he grabbed it. At least it was *that* useful.

"I see you've put on more muscle in the past few years. You're still as gorgeous as I remember." Tymon ran a hand over my chest and stomach before giving my cock a few tugs. "I've missed you."

"I'm truly sorry for how I treated you," I said.

He released me. "Do you expect that will make everything better?"

"No, I don't," I said. "Nothing can ever take away the pain I've caused you. What I did was heartless and cruel, and you didn't deserve it. You were a good man whose only mistake was falling for a selfish ass."

"Your pretty words still don't change anything." He tilted his head to the side. "Well, if I'm not mistaken, we're about to have company."

As soon as the words were out of his mouth, the wall to my left buckled and crashed into the room in a shower of stones, dust, and one pissed off dragon. I don't which was louder—the wall's death or Kradyn's roar.

"Oh, yes, very impressive." Tymon waved a hand and the wall rebuilt itself.

Kradyn, now in human form, stalked forward. "You have something that belongs to me, sorcerer, and I've come to reclaim it."

Tymon spoke, and Kradyn stopped in his tracks, visibly struggling against an invisible barrier. "Well, Ruldaan, you're certainly moving up in the world. With something that impressive, I can only imagine the sensations you experienced."

"Please stop this," I said. "There's no need for it."

"There is every need!" Tymon shouted. "You played me for a fool. You fucked me and forgot me when another man came along. You ignored me and treated me like trash thrown in the street. I will have my retribution on you and anyone you hold dear. I will show you that I am not so easily dismissed."

"I'm going to kill you with my bare hands," Kradyn said. He took a step forward, then another. "I'm over a thousand years old, and you're a scrawny little mage. Who do you think is going to win this?" He took another step.

Tymon lifted his hands, and golden light shot out from his fingertips, striking Kradyn in the chest. Kradyn stumbled back but quickly righted himself and moved forward again.

"Try again," he growled.

"Very well." Tymon pointed at me.

A scream tore itself from my throat. My body burned, and I could have sworn I felt my blood boiling within my veins. The pain suddenly subsided, and then I felt a gash form across my chest. Blood sprayed onto the stone floor, and I sagged, my wrists straining against the metal cuffs holding me up.

"You won't get to me before I kill your precious Ruldaan," Tymon said.

I looked up and saw Kradyn stopped in his tracks. "Destroy him," I said.

Kradyn shook his head. "He won't kill you if I submit."

"He'll kill you instead," I said.

"Oh, by the gods, you two are sickening. Do you honestly love this creature?" Tymon asked me.

"Yes, I do."

All three of us cried out in pain and shock when a golden light blazed from the cylinder on my chest. The light subsided enough to see the scroll tube crack in half and fall to the floor. The glowing paper inside unfurled itself and hovered before my eyes.

A voice that was at once mine and foreign recited the words on the parchment. My manacles melted away, and the beam at my back shattered into a million pieces, none of which did any harm to us.

Tymon looked up at me from his now-prone position on the floor. Golden light poured from his eyes. Within moments, a winged shadow, much like the assassin I'd been cursed with, tore itself from his body and exploded. Tymon fell to the floor, motionless.

I looked down at the gash on my chest, and it mended itself. The light quickly dissipated, and I fell to my knees. Within seconds Kradyn had scooped me into his arms and was speaking frantically.

My fingers pressed gently to his lips stopped the verbal onslaught. "I'm fine. Thank you for coming to rescue me." I kissed him, enjoying the feel of his flesh against mine.

"Let's not make a habit of it," he growled.

"I'll try." I looked at Tymon who was slowly pushing himself to his knees. "We should help him."

"I'm going to kill him," Kradyn said.

"No." I moved so he would put me on the floor. "You saw that he was possessed. I don't know why the spell chose this time to work, but there is a reason. We have to find out what it is."

I kissed Kradyn again and then walked to Tymon. I pulled him to his feet, and he sagged against me. "Take it slowly. How are you feeling?"

"What happened?" He stared at me. "Ruldaan. Oh, Ruldaan, I've missed you. Where have you been?"

"You don't remember?" I asked.

"I just left the castle a few minutes ago when a guard told me you weren't available." He looked around the room. "Where are we?"

"All in due time," I said. "Do you remember placing a curse on Genev?"

His eyes widened. "I would never..." He took a deep breath. "I do remember—now." He muttered a few words. A diaphanous dove formed in the air above him then flew through a window. "The counter spell is cast. I am so sorry. I don't know why I did that."

"You were possessed by something," I said. "It's gone now."

"Thank the gods." He kissed me lightly on the lips. He attempted to kiss me again, but I held him away.

"Tymon, you've been possessed for six years," I said. "We aren't together anymore."

"What? Why?" he asked.

"Because I was stupid, and I hurt you. I'm so very sorry," I said. "Please, forgive me."

"I do."

The room was bathed in golden light once again, and I felt it suffuse my every pore. It flowed from me, into Tymon, and then into Kradyn. It circled around and through us, drawing us closer and closer together.

"This is powerful magic—primeval," Kradyn said. "Something tells me your mage was an ancient dragon, or knew one."

"What is it doing?" I asked.

"It's linking us together, although I don't know why."

"Can it be stopped?" I asked. "Why is this happening?"

Kradyn closed his eyes. "I'm not powerful enough. I don't even want to think what would happen if I tried to stop it."

"I can hear your thoughts," Tymon said.

"That is part of the process," Kradyn said. "Human minds are...strange."

"Well, how do you think I feel thinking about eating pearls?" I asked. "Oh, gods!"

Kradyn threw his head back and roared while Tymon and I screamed. The burning sensation suffusing us wasn't nearly as painful as Tymon's spell had been, but it still hurt.

"How do we make this stop?" I shouted.

"I have a suspicion," Tymon said.

"What? Anything. This just has to stop," I said.

Tymon pulled me into a kiss.

Chapter Eleven

J pushed Tymon away. "Stop. No. I'm with Kradyn. I know what I did to you was wrong, but I can't do this."

Tymon screamed and fell on the floor. If I hadn't been able to feel his pain, I would have thought he was being theatrical, but I was on my knees, too, and my head felt like it was going to explode.

Kradyn cradled me much like he had the first time we met. Stroking sweat-soaked hair off my brow he said, "We have no choice. If we don't do this, the spell is going to kill us. There's nothing we can do except what the magic demands."

"But I love you," I said.

He smiled and kissed me gently. "And I love you. Nothing will change that, but we have to do this. There's a reason you were given this spell. There's a reason it's so powerful and binding the three of us together. We have to trust that all three of us are to be united. Otherwise, we're doomed."

Reaching out, I took Tymon's hand in mine and placed both of them in Kradyn's massive palm. The heat emanating from all of us was almost as overpowering as the spell. I could also hear the thoughts from both Kradyn and Tymon warring inside my head. Desire and the need for release were palpable.

The magic surged, and Tymon threw himself on me, bruising my lips with his. His tongue darted into my mouth, and I relaxed into Kradyn, giving myself to Tymon. Both of them were rubbing my quickly hardening cock.

Tymon tore away the fastenings of my breeches, roughly seizing my erection and stroking it. "I've missed having you inside me," he whispered against my mouth. "Fuck me, Ruldaan." He glanced up at Kradyn. "And I want you to fuck me, too, dragon."

Kradyn looked at me, and I nodded. "Gladly," he growled, causing Tymon's grip on me to tighten.

I sat forward, pushing Tymon back. "Let's get you out of those robes." I laughed when he quickly stripped them over his head, exposing his nakedness and an engorged shaft so hard it could shatter stone.

Without warning, I swallowed Tymon's cock, pressing my nose against his flesh. I cupped his balls, gently squeezing them. Kradyn moved around behind him, spreading his ass cheeks apart and diving into the crevice. The sounds of his slurping and licking at the tight ring urged me on and were in strict competition with the moans and whimpers we elicited from Tymon.

Continuing to suck on Tymon, I pulled the globes of his firm ass apart, giving Kradyn easier, unfettered access to the feast before him.

"What is it with you humans and your wonderfully tight holes?" Kradyn said when he came up for air. "It's maddening!" He dived back in.

"I need someone in me," Tymon begged. "I don't care who, just as long as I have my ass filled. Now!"

His cock slid from my throat, sprang upward, and slapped against his toned stomach with a wet slap that echoed from the walls. I barely gave Kradyn time to remove his face before I spun Tymon around, bent him over, and positioned myself at the event horizon of his hole.

"All the way in," Tymon said.

I obliged. Kradyn had made a sloppy, wet mess of him, and I used that to our advantage. Without hesitation, I pushed into Tymon and didn't stop until my balls met his. He groaned when I immediately pulled completely out and slammed fully into him again, repeating the process several times.

His shouts and begging for more became muffled then silenced when Kradyn filled him from the other end. We had him skewered between us, and the thoughts flooding all our minds ratcheted up the sensations.

"Move aside," Kradyn ordered.

I thrust into Tymon twice more before pulling out and stepping back, giving Kradyn access. He wasted no time pushing the head of his massive cock into Tymon, but he did resist the urge of pushing all the way in. I feared Tymon would have died if Kradyn had done that.

"You're so tight," Kradyn said.

"By the gods, you're huge," Tymon panted. "I want it all."

Kradyn laughed. "Then all you shall have." He pushed slowly forward, giving Tymon the ability to relax and welcome the invader like a lost lover.

I kneeled before Tymon, kissing him. "Are you sure you want this?"

He nodded. I knew from my own experience what he was feeling. To help put his mind on other things, I moved beneath him and resumed my efforts to empty his balls. He gasped and rocked forward then back, pleasuring himself in two places at once.

"That's all in," Kradyn said. "Good man. Only you and Ruldaan have ever fully taken me."

Tymon gasped. "It feels amazing. Stay all the way inside me." He focused on his breathing while reaching down and playing two fingers in a circle around my hole.

"Ruldaan, come back here," Kradyn ordered.

I left off Tymon again and moved beside Kradyn. He kissed me, forcing his tongue into my mouth while he slowly started rocking back and forth. His cock was barely moving in and out of Tymon's stretched hole, and from his thoughts, I knew it was driving him insane. He wanted to unleash his full fury.

"You need to be inside me," he said.

I wasted no time fulfilling the command. Rubbing a large glob of spittle onto my member, followed my one smeared onto his waiting hole, I pushed inside. Kradyn immediately thrust backward, impaling himself on me while pulling partially out of Tymon. He reversed momentum and continued rebounding between us.

"I'm cumming," Tymon shouted. The force of his orgasm ripped through all of us, setting off a tidal wave of cum. Tymon painted the floor white. Kradyn's massive load of seed filled Tymon's abused ass to overflowing, and his orgasm milked me dry.

We collapsed into the floor in a heap of still-joined sweaty flesh. Kradyn didn't stop fucking Tymon until he had added a second load to the first. When he pulled out of Tymon, the sorcerer whimpered, and I could feel the sense of emptiness suffuse me.

"I can't wait to do that again," Tymon said.

Kradyn laughed. "Give me a few minutes, and I will gladly fuck that amazing hole again."

"Me first," I said, smacking his ass with my palm.

Before Kradyn could respond, a roaring wind blew through the door at the far end of the room, propelling splinters of wood onto the floor. A bluish-gray mist creeped across the stones and slowly formed into a column that finally coalesced into a man I'd not seen in years.

"Your Majesty." The ghostly Grand Magus bowed before me. His foggy eyes swept up and locked onto mine, sending chills down my spine. "I have been summoned because you have used the spell."

"What is the purpose of the spell?" I asked. I stood to face him so I could give my knees a rest from the hard stone floor. Kradyn supported Tymon as they stood beside me.

"I was never one for prognostication," the ghost said. "However, the only time I was able to see into the future, I saw the three of you facing a terrible evil the likes of which the world has never known. Due to the nature of this force, I knew that you three must be bound together in mind and spirit, or else you would all perish."

"But how did you know about the shadow assassin and the spirit possessing Tymon?" I asked.

"I didn't," the ghost said. "I knew nothing other than the fact the three of you must be one. Everything else is negligible."

"What can you tell us of this threat?" Kradyn asked.

"Nothing. I'm sorry. All I saw was the three of you falling before it," he said. "I knew the spell would offer you some protection. I wish I could tell you more."

"How can we stand against something we know nothing about?" Tymon asked.

"I have no answer to your questions. However, I can give you one last bit of assistance." The room once again filled with howling wind, and the ghost shimmered briefly before separating into three separate parts.

The mist quickly closed the distance between the three of us, and we all fell to the floor when it slammed into us. I heard the former mage's voice in my head, whispering secrets I couldn't fathom or remember.

"When it is time, all will be revealed." The words echoed in my skull and in the room. The wind receded, and the destroyed door reformed and appeared to have no blemishes at all.

Epilogue

$\mathcal{I}$ sat on my throne, overlooking the assemblage of court officials in colorful attire. I smiled at Genev sitting next to me, and she returned the gesture while grasping Prince Zadron's hand.

The weight of Kradyn's hand on my shoulder forced me to look up at him, and he kissed me softly while ensuring my crown didn't fall from my head. Beside us, Mother made a noise, but she was unable to hide her smile.

The Lord Chamberlain announced Tymon moments before the entry doors opened. The second part of my heart strode purposefully forward, pointedly ignoring the whispers the ebbed and flowed through the sea of onlookers. At the base of the dais, he dropped to one knee and stared at the floor.

"Rise, Tymon, and look upon your king," I commanded.

He stood, and his eyes darted from me to Genev to Mother and then back to me. "Your Majesties, I stand before you today to accept punishment for my actions which have caused such grievous injury to you all."

The whispers became louder until I raised my hand to put a stop to them. Tymon looked back at the floor, and I could tell he was clenching his hands inside the sleeves of his robe.

"How did you come to be possessed by the spirit?" I asked.

"I don't know, Your Majesty," he said, looking up at me. "I have no recollection of any spells gone awry or of handling any artifact that might have caused me to become possessed."

"And you have no memory of casting the spells upon me or Genev? Or of committing murder?"

Tymon fell to his knees. He was so pale I feared he might either lose consciousness or vomit. I couldn't go to him, but I sent Kradyn, who comforted Tymon as much as possible. Everyone—

including me—was shocked when Mother descended the steps and kneeled on the floor before Tymon.

After several minutes of hushed conversation, Mother and Kradyn helped Tymon to his feet and stood on either side of him as he faced me again.

Genev nodded slightly when I looked at her, and then I stood to make my pronouncement. "Tymon, the crown absolves you of all charges against your King and the Princess Genev. As for the murder of Sir Jullain, we must find you guilty. However, due to the circumstances surrounding the murder, and due to the fact Sir Jullain has no living family, you are ordered to pay two thousand gold pieces to the royal treasury."

I left the throne and stood before Tymon and Kradyn, thanking Mother for being supportive. I knew it wasn't easy for her, but after I'd explained the situation—and knowing Genev was fully recovered—she had relented to my wishes.

Mother, Genev, and Zadron left before the gathered lords and ladies, who quickly filed out, leaving the three of us alone.

"How are you?" I asked Tymon.

He sighed. "I'll be better eventually. It's just difficult to face so many people who know the evil things I have done but can't remember. Thank you for your support."

I took his hands in mine and kissed him. "You're welcome. I'm just glad that we are together again—all of us." I kissed Kradyn, too.

"I need to leave. I'm sorry, but I don't think I can be here right now," Tymon said.

"Well, as luck would have it, I've already planned a trip for us," I said.

"Where?" Tymon asked.

"My cave," Kradyn responded.

"What are we going to do there?" Tymon asked.

Kradyn winked at him. "Don't worry. We'll think of something."

Cover Design by:

TatteredWolf Studios is the joint venture of husband and wife team Brad and Megan Baker (otherwise known as Loni and Tatiyana Wolf). The goal of TWS is to bring their unique design aesthetic to the world through traditional, digital, and video game art.

They can be found at www.TatteredWolfStudios.com.